MISHMASH

Alex Vorn

BALBOA.
PRESS

A DIVISION OF HAY HOUSE

Balboa Press books may be ordered through booksellers or by contacting:

Balboa Press
A Division of Hay House
1663 Liberty Drive
Bloomington, IN 47403
www.balboapress.com.au
1 (877) 407-4847

Because of the dynamic nature of the Internet, any web addresses or
links contained in this book may have changed since publication and
may no longer be valid. The views expressed in this work are solely those
of the author and do not necessarily reflect the views of the publisher,
and the publisher hereby disclaims any responsibility for them.

The author of this book does not dispense medical advice or prescribe the use
of any technique as a form of treatment for physical, emotional, or medical
problems without the advice of a physician, either directly or indirectly. The
intent of the author is only to offer information of a general nature to help
you in your quest for emotional and spiritual well-being. In the event you use
any of the information in this book for yourself, which is your constitutional
right, the author and the publisher assume no responsibility for your actions.

Any people depicted in stock imagery provided by Thinkstock are
models, and such images are being used for illustrative purposes only.
Certain stock imagery © Thinkstock.

Printed in the United States of America.

ISBN: 978-1-4525-2533-4 (sc)
ISBN: 978-1-4525-2534-1 (e)

Balboa Press rev. date: 09/12/2014

Dedicated to Mary, Jasmine and Leanne

Contents

The Puzzlements

The puzzlements that are, and need no seeking out,
The natural profusions abundant here,
Are quest enough, for any soul,
To find full occupation (not withstanding much elation)
In what he may, through his own choice,
Learn to see or hear.

And from these teaming aspects we
May individualise an act,
And separate its plot through time
To build upon the fact.

And thus, we take winter-time,
In which our aspect holds.
A single, fleeting puzzlement
Of this plot's own true wonderment
And so our act unfolds.

Super soft flecks of silver ice
Swirling through golden labyrinths of sun-spent rays,
Falling through leafy canopies
To touch, soft white, the floor of this,
Our own earthly maze.

And on it goes, and on and on.
These puzzles do not cease.
For with the looking and the seeing,
Do they not increase?

To The Poets

To all those here and around the world
Who share the poet's lot.
To those who know the ebb and flow
Of note, and word,
Of song, and play, and plot.

The words that are often for others to speak,
Through the rhythm and rhyme of verse.
The thoughts and ideas that can swamp the mind,
And often seem like a curse.

To all who have struggled with such strife,
To all who have been and returned,
May your courage remain, through each laboured refrain,
And may you each know the joy that is earned.

To Draw the Line

I met a man on the six o'clock train out of the city.

The memory of that journey will always be vivid. I often think back to that evening, climbing into the waiting carriage, and the events that followed. I can easily recall the lingering warmth of the day, the gathering rain clouds, the sleep inducing noise of the clickety-clack as the train got underway, and the murky views from the carriage; views not changing fast enough to hold my interest. The train hadn't been moving very long when the novelty of staring out of the window wore off. With little else to do, I began to study the only other passenger.

A man in his fifties maybe, well dressed, neat, professional. I got the impression from his general demeanour that the humdrum of the rocking carriage was getting to him as well. It wasn't long before we struck up idle conversation.

It was quickly established that occupationally, we were worlds apart. My attempts at producing a manuscript good enough to get into paperback didn't stack up really well against his being a geneticist. This apparent disparity wasn't a problem for my companion. He was obviously glad of the diversion.

The "DNA thing" had fascinated me ever since a neighbour had undergone testing as part of some student programme at a local university. With the usual tenacity of someone who gets a kick out of reading up on subjects, whether the stuff is destined to become a book or not, I delved into the mind-boggling enormity of it all, until the novelty deserted me. But this was not before reading two rather impressive articles on the global Human Genome Project.

I had found that the progress made in the research and study of genetic material of organisms fascinating, and yet somehow disturbing. The concept of what the scientists had called the functional units of inheritance was both appealing and unsettling at the same time.

After a reasonable amount of time chatting about the usual things, of little or no consequence, I said I would appreciate the opportunity to confirm a few facts with him on the subject of the ongoing project.

"Sure, no problem", he said.

We both adjusted ourselves in our seats and he said, "Okay, what questions do you have?"

"First", I began, "I'd like to confirm that our DNA exists in every cell in our bodies, which I understand is about sixty trillion cells?"

"Sixty trillion? Is that how many cells we have?" He smiled, "Yes. Almost all of our cells, with some exceptions, have the identical DNA."

"And might one visualise the forty-six chromosomes that form our DNA as each one being a separate thread".

"A thread? Sure, why not. We have used the term 'string', but it amounts to the same thing."

He took a moment to pluck some loose material from the frayed edge of his seat, went through a brief sorting process, and then held something up before his face. "Yeah, this is about right and it's about two inches long, which is the length of a chromosome. Of course, they're all tightly coiled so you'd have to stretch one out to make it look like this."

"So, that comes to about ninety-two inches or almost eight feet of thread if you were to connect them all together and draw them out in a straight line."

"Interesting idea, yes, you could look at it like that."

I took the thread from his hand and asked, "As I understand it, if this thread was actually a DNA chromosome, it would be so thin it would actually be invisible to the naked eye."

"Quite correct. It's not only invisible to the naked eye; it's invisible to some of our strongest electron microscopes. It actually takes sophisticated X-Ray equipment to examine these 'threads' as you call them. Nowadays, the most modern equipment uses lasers."

"Now the term 'gene', as I understand it, applies to sections of this eight-foot thread of DNA, just imagining that this thread is eight-feet long," I said, dangling the thread he had given me, between us. "Is that correct?"

"Yes, and the commonly held notion that there are approximately 100,000 genes is only a method for classifying sections of the thread."

"Okay, now here's the hard part, which I have to tell you I find difficult to comprehend."

"Go ahead, test me." The man looked a little smug.

"Well, as I understand it, there are actually twenty billion bits of information on this DNA thread, which converts to about three billion letters, of which there are only four. Four different types, that is."

"Four letters, you mean."

"Yes."

"What you say is all quite true. There are approximately three billion copies of four letters encoded on our imaginary string or thread of DNA, each one representing one of four proteins, which are the building blocks of everything in our bodies. Amazing, isn't it?"

"To say the least. And I read that under the Human Genome Project, which is currently underway, scientists worldwide are literally copying the sequence of letters on this thread and when they are through, sometime during this first decade of the new millennium they think, there will be the equivalent of 300,000 pages of letters. That's if it were set in the typeface used in a standard encyclopaedia."

"Sounds about right. I've seen the coding referred to as the equivalent of four hundred volumes of the Encyclopaedia Britannica."

"All this, from this one eight-foot thread." I waved the little thread in the air.

"Yes, yes, quite correct."

"And these letters are the basic coding for the human body."

"Yes, in the sense that without them there wouldn't be a human body!"

"Now is it true", I continued, "that as our cells divide, each of those 3 billion letters are replicated?"

"Oh, yes, it is quite a complex process."

"Now I read this somewhere and it's sort of mind-boggling, is it true that before the cells divide, little checkers, so to speak, go down each of the new DNA threads to make sure the replication is accurate, and if mistakes are spotted, these checkers can actually fix them?"

"Checkers, did you say?"

"Yes, checkers."

The scientist broke out laughing. "You know, he continued, you certainly have a way of reducing the most complex processes to an embarrassing level of simplicity."

"Yes, but it took a lot of time poring through books to figure out that the enzymes that do the job are really little checkers and that they can cut out and repair mistakes on the DNA that is being replicated."

"Yes, in essence that is what the enzymes do."

"Then I learned that our cells divide at different rates, with some dividing in under two hours. So this whole process of creating a 300,000-page volume of human coding can be done that quickly, and with checkers making sure those sequences of letters were all copied correctly. Can you confirm that what I am saying is true?"

"Oh. Yes, it's true all right."

I looked blankly at him and added, "So the Great Architect has to be some kind of top-gun design engineer."

"Great Architect?"

"You know, the fellow upstairs." I pointed to the carriage's ceiling.

He laughed again, "Yes indeed, someone had to be an engineer beyond all comprehension to design this system."

I sat staring at the floor of the carriage for a while.

"Run out of questions?"

"No. Not really, I need to draw a line."

The man looked puzzled, "You need what?"

"I just wanted to mark out eight feet, it might be a little easier for my brain to register these facts."

"Well, go ahead. I take it you don't carry a tape measure?"

"No, I'll use my shoe-lengths, they're about twelve inches long."

I got up, steadying myself against the rocking of the compartment and paced out about eight feet. I took a couple of coins from my pocket. With these placed at either end of my imaginary thread, I sat back down.

"There", I said. "Now, as I see it, the similarity between my invisible thread and your thread of DNA chromosomes, is that if yours were all connected together like this it would be just invisible to the human eye and some of our strongest microscopes. But, it would be ultimately visible."

"Okay, I accept your observation on that."

"The real difference being that although they are both invisible to all intents and purposes, mine doesn't exist but it has been proven that yours does."

The man smiled and nodded.

"Yet every organ in our body is encoded into the three billion letters on this invisible thread?"

"That is correct."

"Including our brain, the most complex object in the known universe."

"Well, yes, including our brain, this by the way takes up in the neighbourhood of a third of all those letters."

"Now, in the photographic reproductions I've seen of DNA the four basic letters are represented by markings that look like bar codes."

"Bar codes?"

"Yes, you know, the bar codes on packets of corn flakes and tins of baked beans and the like, that get scanned at check-out counters in supermarkets."

He thought a moment and then smiled yet again. He was obviously enjoying this conversation. "They do look like those bar codes, don't they?"

"So it wouldn't be inaccurate to say that all of human life emanates from a series of bar codes."

"Well then, yes, you could say that we all come from a series of bar codes."

"All classified neatly on this eight-foot string of thread."

"Yes."

"Which, in the laboratory, might one day be cloned to produce a human being."

The man shifted a little, clasping his hands on his lap.

"Yes, the possibility exists for that to happen."

"So, this means the possibility exists that we might one day be able to clone each of the sixty trillion cells in our body and find that we are able to create human beings. Lots more human beings, in a world running out of resources, including food! Enough, as it were, to entirely swamp the planet! Who will be the one to say 'start', who is going to say 'stop', who will draw the line?"

I looked through the darkening window. I pictured a world where science had taken over. A world where it, in its cleverness, had convinced the masses that it was on the right track, then run riot with humanity. A world teeming with starving people.

These images were still racing through my mind as I glanced back into the swaying compartment.

The man looked far less at ease now. He looked up and shrugged his shoulders.

Had I gone too far?

I hadn't wanted to upset my companion. I have been told before that I don't know when or where to draw the line. Despite knowing all this, I decided it was too late to turn back. After all I had every right to make my point. I decided to push on.

"But one day", I continued, as politely as I could, "that might be a possibility."

"I can't deny that. No, in all honesty I can't."

I stood up and swept my hand over the imaginary line across the floor, "So this thread is composed of three billion letters formed in bar codes and this is what human life is made of."

"Not only human life, he replied becoming amused again, but all organic life. The only difference between that string on the floor and one for a cat, a kangaroo, an owl, a flea, an apricot or a flower's petal is its length and the configuration of letters."

"So all life forms emanate from this same thread full of bar codes?"

"Yes, you could say that."

Including you, me, and the person driving this train. They all came from threads like these.'

"Yes, a string of DNA, whose polymorphisms, if you'll excuse the technical term, create the differences between individuals."

"Including mental differences, the variances of the software in our brains that makes each of us not only look different, but think and act differently."

"Yes, I would imagine so."

"And this string of DNA, this thread, hasn't changed much in the past 50,000 years and so what I'm looking at here could just as easily have belonged to a caveman as to Adolph Hitler."

"Well, I'm no anthropologist, but you can assume that the DNA string hasn't changed very much since humans first became humans."

"So, what you are saying is that the predispositions of our every instinct, including the very instinct of survival itself, are all encoded onto this eight foot thread." It wasn't meant to be a question, but a statement.

My companion obviously took it as a question anyway and stared out into what had become night.

Again. Had I said too much?

I stared at the two coins and the invisible line they drew.

We both sat in silence for some time. He finally roused himself as the train began to slow. As he stood gathering his belongings from the overhead rack he looked a little weary. I hadn't noticed this before.

He sat down again briefly and said, "All I can tell you is that the structure of the brain is definitely encoded on the DNA, so whatever your brain includes when it first comes out of the womb is a result of that coding. As for these other points you raised, well, I can't really comment on those. After all, I'm a gene man, not a brain man!"

The scientist was no longer at ease. He glanced somewhat nervously around the compartment, as if looking for things left behind.

He opened the door and got out. I followed.

As we walked through the station building I tried to make amends by thanking him for his time. He turned and said, "Well, you know what they say, don't call me, I'll call you." The man tried very hard to smile, before disappearing into the noise and gloom of the waiting city.

As I watched him hail a taxi, I was aware of an empty, unsatisfied feeling deep within the pit of my stomach.

I was left with the thought that when you get right down to the very essence of being human, we are just the result of an enormous number of bar codes that are responsible for growing our bodies and our brains.

I often think of that journey. The man, the ideas, the questions left unanswered. In times of trouble, I often revert to the thought that I am nothing more than an eight foot string of DNA, which had somehow became fertilised into a temporary human, who lives on a planet that is lost somewhere in space.

Mark you; I only do this when I really need comforting.

The Wind

Whistling, floating, swooping and soaring,
Hissing, moaning, hooting and roaring.
Across the fields it ripples and scatters,
Along the roofs it rumbles and clatters.

The trees must bend, and leaves must fly,
As the howl from the forest must blend with a sigh.
The current of a stream hastens or slows,
Showing from which direction it blows.

Leaves and such can climb and loop,
While others prefer to dive and swoop.
Things of the ground may roll and smash,
While others would rather topple and crash.

It comes in a puff, a gust, or a breeze,
Sometimes a scream, a sob, or a wheeze;
But whether it's there to harm or please,
It's surely a mystery that nobody sees.

Great Time

Great Time — come and go, to and fro,
And shed the tears of those
That would not cry before their time,
But rather you did trundle on
And toll the bell and make them gone.

It's left to you. All's left to you.
No meddling hand effects
The cutting sweep of your mighty scythe
Within the harvest of one life
That makes all things alive.

No boundaries there, no laws to break.
And freedom is to you, as would be
For a jailer, who, with mouths to feed
Did bar the world with cunning greed,
Behind his prison gate.

We do not fight, we take our place,
And humbly live our span.
But never would this one thing stop a living soul
From searching in his mind; to free his kind,
From that which impales man.

For The Time Being

It was two o'clock in the morning when Troy looked at his watch. A quarter of an hour to go, if their calculations were right. He peered through the drizzle and down the road. He could hardly see a thing in the dark, but he knew the German soldiers were down there, about 200 yards away. They were waiting for the same man. Well, this time they wouldn't get him.

Water dripped off his hat and down his neck. The cold seeped into his bones but he hardly noticed the discomfort. The silence was unnerving. The danger and tension were like a drug to him, and he couldn't imagine living without it.

Saving lives of long dead soldiers seemed rather futile, but it was all experimentation, he knew that. Thank goodness these back-room boffins, with their strange ideas about how to gauge the long-term effects of time travel and manipulating the past, were hard at work on his behalf.

He thought about the complexity of it all. It was mind-boggling. It had taken months to set up tonight's show.

Pierre, the French resistance fighter, the man he was waiting to rescue, would be happy. He was walking into a trap and in a few minutes from now was scheduled to die. As it was, with the wonders of twenty-fifth century technology, he would live to spy another day and a number of British soldiers would now survive a battle they hadn't survived the first time around.

Troy looked carefully down the road. A portly, hunched-over figure in a wide-brimmed hat and wrapped in a long coat was now just visible in the gloom, hurrying along the wet street.

"In here," Troy hissed as he caught the figure by the arm and dragged him into the side alley. "There has been a small change of plan; you're walking into a trap. Come with me."

Pierre caught on quickly. He had to in his job. "I'm in your hands, Monsieur," he whispered back as Troy quietly led him through a series of dimly lit back alleys. They finally stopped at a door; Troy knocked quietly and waited. As the door opened he pushed Pierre through. "Here's your man," he whispered, then hurried away back down the alley.

Moments later Troy stood silently in the pitch-blackness of a doorway, as if in a trance. In fact, he was manipulating a small device in his pocket. His link with his own time. An exact sequence was being performed, followed by the press of a button. After a few moments a wall of grey mist appeared directly in front of him. He took two short steps and passed through it.

-----oOo-----

Troy emerged out if the mist into a room he'd been in countless times before. Brilliant sunshine was trying to get through a high window. He was back at the agency.

A thin, balding man sat at a desk, a folder open in front of him. Troy looked at his boss in his crumpled, grey suit, dusty office with the light struggling to get in. Suits him, thought Troy contemptuously. Grey room, grey man, boring bean-counting job. No love was lost between them and neither man had ever tried to hide the fact. He removed his coat; still dripping with water centuries old, drooped it over the back of a spare chair and sat down at the desk.

"Well?" he asked inquiringly.

Mendler looked up at him. "I hope you enjoyed your final field trip," he said smoothly.

"This won't be my last one, not by a long shot."

"Don't you count on it. I've been doing a little research. You go five weeks forward, come back and start winning large amounts of money on the horses. Very suspicious".

Mendler smiled for the first time that Troy could remember.

"We're also investigating your investments on the stock market. One of them has paid off quite handsomely already I believe. I have to tell you that the Government, and this Institution, take a very serious view of using information gained in the future to make a profit in the present. It could undermine our entire financial system. By the time my report goes in you'll never work for this organisation or the Government again. But don't worry; you won't need a job where you're going. And you'll have your associate Mister Dawson for company."

Troy went cold inside. He kept his face impassive. "Dawson, an associate of mine? You're barking up the wrong tree. Now, if you've finished counting your unhatched chickens, maybe you could tell me how well we did this time."

"Ah, yes, a total success", he said grudgingly. "You obviously delivered the agent to the Resistance, as his information was passed on to Allied Intelligence. The immediate result was that we won a minor battle several days after you were there, and we estimate we saved the lives of 20 British soldiers. The longer-term results are still being calculated. We would normally let you know more details as they come to hand, but that will only happen if you are still around".

"I'll still be here."

"I can only repeat, I wouldn't count on it. I've had my eye on you for a while. I knew your greed would get the better of you one day. You know, it's remarkable how your friend Dawson has made such astute investments over the last few months. His new technology company is bringing out some interesting inventions as well. And it's all happened since you started travelling forwards in time. An amazing coincidence, don't you think?"

Troy didn't answer. He grabbed his coat and left. It was time to meet with his partner. A thing they avoided doing too often.

-----oOo-----

Dawson was used to the direct approach. A stocky, tough man, he'd used the direct approach to become one of the richest men in the city. He had the sort of business the weak didn't survive in, and neither did people with scruples.

"We'll have to get rid of this Mendler," he growled. "By the time we've finished with him, no one will be game enough to pick up where he left off. They'll know exactly what will happen to them. It's worked before, and it'll work again." Intimidation and making people disappear were his specialty.

Troy had a different approach in mind.

"The way I see it, Mendler hates my guts, and he'll use this to get rid of me if he can. The cops hate your guts, and they'll use this to get rid of you. Between them they could put us away forever. But I don't want to get mixed up with murder if we can come up with something better."

Dawson laughed. "The cops have tried to get me before, but if no one will testify, or be found to give evidence, what can they do? Mendler's an idiot."

"He may be an idiot, but he's like a ferret. Obviously he's been doing a lot of checking, and he's very confident. No one else would have worried about a few wins on the horses or even making a few dollars on the stock market. He did though, and that could lose me my job, and that's bad enough. Somehow he's made the connection between us. I don't know how, but he's done it. We've made a fortune with the information I've brought back. He may be an idiot, but he's a clever idiot. When his report is sent up the line they'll lock us up and throw away the key."

"We'll just get rid on him," Dawson repeated. "Then there'll be no problem."

Troy had spent ten years changing history with more subtle methods. "No. There's a better way. I guess I've been half expecting something like this. I've got a plan, and if we pull it off, we're on easy street for the rest of our lives."

"What we do is stop time travel being discovered, then we discover it ourselves, and build our own machine. We could go forwards, get all the information we need, and make a killing without anyone knowing what we are doing. We bring back all the racing results, all the stock market results, and whatever technology we wanted, and no one would have any idea of what was going on."

Dawson could see the possibilities. "It sounds good. Convince me. Tell me how we're going to do it."

"This is how we change history," Troy said. "We make small changes that have big effects."

Troy leaned forward, resting his elbows on the table and looked Dawson in the eye.

"Right." he said. "This is how we deal with Mendler and the cops, and anyone else who tries to stick their noses in."

"As we all know, the principles of time travel were discovered by Phillip Greenburg. He was a mathematician, and that's the only reason he had the knowledge to do it. He became a mathematician because he went to Monkton University, where he was strongly influenced by one of the professors. So this is what we do. We get him to go to Bosworth University. Their emphasis is on computer science, and Greenburg was interested in that. Then, he becomes a computer scientist, not a mathematician, and doesn't discover time travel."

"Okay, we stop him discovering it, but how do we discover it?"

Troy opened his case and took out a box of disks. "I've been busy. This is all the information on time travel. It's got Greenburg's original formulae and theorems. I have all the theory we need to 'discover' time travel, and all the engineering information we need to build a working machine right here on these disks."

"We get Greenburg to go to Bosworth and become a computer scientist by making a small but very important change. The reason he went to Monkton was because he couldn't afford the fees at Bosworth."

"Now, I've done some digging into Greenberg's private life. At the time he applied to Monkton he was driving an old Bradley Turbo Tourer. The car itself wasn't worth much, but there weren't many of them left on the road. My plan is to go back to his time, a few days before he put in his application. I show up, announcing myself as a Bradley buff, with more money than I know what to do with. I offer him a wad of money for his old bomb. He sells it, uses the money to apply to Bosworth, never goes to Monkton, and never discovers time travel."

Troy studied Dawson, who had sat quietly taking it all in. "What do you think?"

Dawson grinned. "Do it," he said.

-----ooo------

A sense of intense excitement swept over Troy as he stood in his apartment fingering the device in his pocket. A wall of mist appeared. He stepped through.

-----ooo-----

Troy stood across the street from Greenberg's house. He had made a call and found the car-owner more than willing to part with his vehicle, especially for the figure mentioned.

What he was about to do would change history. It would make him the most powerful man in the world, and the richest! He could not afford to make any mistakes. Everything had to be done with the sort of precision that the last several years working as a time operative with the agency had taught him.

He took a deep breath and started across the street.

With all his past experience, it was remarkable that he didn't see the car take the corner too fast and wander across the white line. He heard it, but he didn't see it. Troy was spun in the air like a rag doll, coming down with a thud in the middle of the road. The pain that wracked his body was almost more than he could stand. He was about to pass out when he saw something on the ground in front of him that froze his blood.

His time device was only a metre away.

With enormous effort he began to straighten his arm. He moved the angle of his head to get a better view, just in time to see the wheels of a vehicle crush the device. He lay looking at the broken pieces of plastic and circuit board, trying very hard to comprehend what all this meant to him, personally. It all seemed to be too much to take in.

People were gathering at the scene. He heard voices drifting in and out while a medic checked him over. A man was talking to a police officer.

"Greenberg, yes I live just over there, I think he was coming to see me. Well, he rang me earlier you see. Said he was interested in my car. It's a Bradley, you know. Anyway, he said he would arrive about now. I was looking out of my front window when I saw the car hit him."

The officer said something about identification.

"No. Sorry officer," replied Greenberg, "he didn't give his name. No. No idea where he's from. He's a keen car collector apparently."

As someone who had spent a lot of time going in and out of the future, Troy started to consider his own.

All in all, it didn't look very good.

This Thing

This thing that never ceases to amaze,
This power born not to die,
The light of which will always daze,
The likes of you or I.

This triumph and this glory
All bound in one idea,
That spurs we simple mortals to
A sigh, a laugh, a tear.

This weapon that fights all battles,
Against evil, foe, or fear.
This true wonder that a few possess,
That's always very near.

This blessing that commands our lives,
That none can rise above.
This hope for which, each man strives;
This jewel, this key, this love.

How long?

How long may youth's wild beauty stay?
How long the day of wonder last?
How long can the freshness of its awe
Hold that impetuous mind that before
Would roam and scan with mischievous glee,
That uncertain world of immaturity?

How long now must it be before,
Even if unwillingly,
The curtain of time falls without tact,
Bringing to close this era, this act?
Surely it seems no uncertain timing
That brings the lowering of that dreaded cloth.
But rather the inevitability, such as the death,
By candles flame,
Of that poor, yet foolish moth.

If then, our time is called and marked,
And through it, we in crowds are marched,
Then we surely each must make our youths a precious task.
And to this end must work,
Never once to stop and ask
A fellow marcher on the way.
How long may youth's wild beauty stay?

Reflections

A tiny bell from the dresser gave out ten o'clock as Jill went into her bedroom. As she entered she paused and gazed across the room. She had begun to hate her mirror.

Each time she looked into it her reflection seemed a little older. Once ebony hair fell about her slim shoulders, now the ebony had turned partly to grey and her hair was twisted into a tight knot and pinned high on her head. She peered at the lines in her brow that deepened with the frown at their very presence. Tracks of time she called them, a reminder that the years had passed by too quickly. Why did all this seem so important now, she pondered? Perhaps because all her friends had children and grandchildren to visit on weekends, leaving her alone with her thoughts and endless paperbacks. So much romance and adventure, all in her own room; lost loves found with just the turn of a page.

She sighed. "If only..." she said aloud as a vision of Rodney manifested itself in her mind. Rodney, forever young. She couldn't visualise him with wrinkles and grey hair, not Rodney.

The night was still, and the scent of honeysuckle greeted Jill as she stepped from the verandah of her tiny cottage.

Perhaps Jack's Cafe might still be open; cinnamon toast and hot chocolate would certainly brighten a dull Saturday night.

Jack waved as she entered and made her way to a table.

"And how is the lovely Miss Baker tonight?" He asked with a note of mischief in his voice. "And what is madam's pleasure?"

Jill laughed. "Now you stop that Jack, people will start to talk." She gave him her order and glanced around the cafe as he strode off to the kitchen.

It was a small and homely establishment, not really popular with the teenage set who preferred the milk bar on the corner. But to Jill it had a feeling of belonging, with its crisp white tablecloths and blue velvet drapes. It seemed untouched by the outside world. Jack had always kept a good house and a good clientele.

The sound of voices came from behind her and she looked up at the mirror running the length of the wall. She could see a young couple engrossed in animated discussion. Their voices grew more intense and the woman seemed close to tears. Jill squirmed a little knowing she should look away from this intimate scene, but something was drawing her into it, something so familiar it almost made her cry out.

"I can't," the woman was saying. "I just cannot marry you." She toyed with the string of pearls at her throat and avoided the pleading eyes of her companion. He reached across the table and brushed back a strand of her ebony hair in danger of escaping its silver clasp. "All I ask is forgiveness," he said.

The woman shook her head and began to rise as if to leave but her arm was grasped and held firmly.

Jill sat transfixed as though watching a rerun of a familiar movie and knowing the outcome. She wanted to turn away from the events unfolding before her, but something held her spellbound.

The man's tone grew hard and cynical as he spoke. "Just one mistake, and you want to give up a lifetime with me. What sort of cold hearted person are you?"

The woman hesitated, caught between the past and future. She began to cry softly, dabbing at her eyes with a lace handkerchief. "It's over." She said finally, putting the wisp of lace in her handbag and closing the clasp with a loud snap.

Jill sat up straight and stared unashamedly into the mirrored scene. This was not the way it was supposed to happen. The woman should run crying from the cafe to spend her life wondering what might have been. Instead she rose and straightened folds of her dress, looked down for a moment at the fine features of her young suitor as though engraving his image in her mind. She took a deep breath and shook her head.

"The fact is I really don't need you any more Rodney," she told him. "One day I'll find someone who loves me, and me alone. In the meantime you can go your own way, but without me." She turned swiftly on her heel and walked out into the night without looking back.

The playing out of this scene had a profound effect on Jill. A sense of enormous relief swept over her like a hot shower. She opened her eyes to take in the comforting surroundings.

"Here we go Miss Baker." Jack placed her order on the table touched her gently on the shoulder. "Are you all right?"

Jill smiled up at him. "Yes Jack I'm fine. Just chasing a few old ghosts away."

Jack rubbed his square jaw slowly and nodded as though he understood. "Yes. They should be laid to rest if they bother you."

"You are a wise man Jack, and you make the best hot chocolate."

"Best in town," came the humorous boast. "When you've done eating I'll walk you home if I might. It's not safe for a pretty lady out alone."

She looked up at him as though she had never seen him before. "Yes, thank you Jack, I'd like that."

He smiled fondly at her as he turned to go. "Right then. That's a date."

The evening had turned cold when they locked and left the café.

"Jack, did you see that young couple in the cafe when I came in tonight, you know, the ones that were arguing?" Asked Jill, as they strolled arm in arm to her house.

Jack shook his head in reply. "It was a very slow night, just you and old Mrs. Mason who comes by for her herbal tea. I was about to close when you arrived. Why do you ask?"

"Oh nothing. Just me being silly. By the way, when are you going to stop calling me Miss Baker and start calling me Jill?"

He looked her full in the face and smiled his best smile. "Is now soon enough?"

The warmth of Jack's response touched Jill in a place once holding only ghosts of the past. They were gone now, played out in a reflection of time, the way it should have been all those long years ago. She knew in her heart that the face she was looking at would change the rest of her life!

Twilight

Now is the time; when twilight falls,
When wording mouths and fleeting thoughts
Give way to rides upon dusty stars,
And this plot of ours is still.

Now we sleep, we ebb, we flow,
And all there is to come and blow
The cobwebs from our daily time comes in,
And sweeps, and blows all else to nil.

Now is the time, now is the sleep.
But there oh day, another day,
And yet another still.
For we that sleep and rest and flow,
For we that fleet and ride, just so,
May never have our fill.

Golden Sun

Golden sun which lays beneath the steps
and treadings of our ancient piece;

Be still, be still; peace, be still…

Before we can sing, or ere give air to
thoughts that lay below this crust.

Then burn on slow and sweet,

But live not outside thine own eruptions, lest one golden
spit of thought should burst and fly and touch our realm;

Rather it should sleep and groan and burn,

And leave each here

To stand alone.

The Last Dangerous Game

The hallway was dimly lit with only a faint light creeping out from a nearby room. It was late in the evening and a smell of camphor hung in the air. The clock in the hall struck thirteen, an event that went unnoticed by the man seated at the desk. On the face of it this was extremely odd, because he was a man with an obsessive preoccupation with superstitions of every kind.

He had once missed an important meeting because he thought he saw a moth fly through a room in his apartment. Not an ordinary moth, but a white moth. A white moth inside a house, or even trying to enter a house, meant death as far as Sebastian was concerned.

Another time he lay awake all night because he thought he heard the tapping sound made by a Death Watch Beetle, which for him foretold of a death in the house.

Anyone meeting Sebastian in his place of work or up at the local shops would never guess that he harboured such compulsive thoughts. He would be regarded as a regular person, maybe a little dull, and certainly not remarkable in any way. He was quiet and unassuming, but always polite.

He lived quietly on his own without bothering anybody. He had no pets and no hobbies to speak of. He rarely went out after working hours and spent most of his evenings sitting at an old desk quietly reading. It would be fair to say that nobody would have suspected him of having a vast knowledge of taboos and omens.

A low buzzing noise came from somewhere across the top of the desk; this also went unnoticed by the man so deeply lost in the pages of his book. The desk and the large, brass reading lamp that adorned it were the only items of any value handed down from his parents. The lamp was especially precious and he went to great pains to keep it polished and free of dust. He would use it as an object of contemplation when he needed to focus his mind on something. It was, without doubt, his most prized possession.

Despite this seemingly dull existence the man at the desk was, in fact, one of the top admen in his business. His spiels, blurbs, musical jingoes and promotional ideas had made his employer's Advertising Agency one of the most successful in the city.

On one occasion, at the agency, a lady had changed her shoes and absent-mindedly left them on the table in the copy-machine room. When Sebastian went in to use the machine he had a very nasty turn. The people in the office were most understanding when he staggered out looking pale and mumbling about not feeling his best, but they didn't know what Sebastian knew. They didn't know that to put shoes on a table signified death by hanging!

Sebastian's mother was single-handledly responsible for the notions that now plagued his adult life. She had a taboo or a superstition to cover every aspect of day-to-day living.

She had said that if you see an ambulance or a hearse you must touch a button or be the next one in it. She had said that if a dog howls at night while facing toward you, you would soon die. She had also said that you would have bad luck if you do not stop the clock in the room where someone dies. She asserted that it was bad luck to meet a funeral procession head on, and that a single snowdrop growing in the garden foretells a death. She also claimed that if a cow 'moos' after midnight, it is an evil omen, and that if you prick your finger on the thorn of a red rose that looks black, you would die. She maintained that a diamond-shaped fold in clean linen portends death, that a hat on the bed means a death in the family, and that if you hold your breath while you pass a cemetery, evil spirits cannot enter your body. She asserted that if an owl looks in through the window of your home during daylight hours, a death would occur in the household!

The list of such sayings seemed to be endless, and Sebastian was weaned on such stuff from the time he could understand what people were saying.

Sebastian turned the page of the book he was reading. As he did, a spider scampered across the desktop and stopped at the base of his desk lamp.

A look of dread came over the man's face. This was a bad sign. Not just the mere fact that it was a spider, but the fact that it had one leg missing! Seeing a seven-legged spider, as his mother had taught him, meant that the person seeing it would die within a day if the spider wasn't killed. Coupled with this, but being of less immediate importance, was the fact that Sebastian hated spiders. Since he was a small boy he had detested them.

As the full impact of the incident, and the importance of destroying the thing dawned on him, the pest disappeared over the edge of the desk.

Sebastian jumped up and ran around the desk, catching his leg on the corner as he went. With raised foot he peered into the shadowy area, waiting for movement. Any movement! But there was none. It had gone. Vanished as though it had never been there! No spider, just a sore leg.

After an hour or more of searching Sebastian slumped back into his chair. He felt exhausted, nauseous and faint. His head collapsed onto his folded arms and he began to sob.

-----ooo------

"I'm going to kill every blessed one of them," he muttered, shoving his way through the door of the hardware store. He grabbed a shopping cart and shot down the centre aisle at breakneck speed; intent on the death and mayhem he had in mind.

He had undergone something of a character change.

"Can I help you?" a salesman said, stepping out in front of him.

"Poison," said Sebastian through clinched lips. Then noting his blank look he clarified. "I need a pesticide."

"Oh. Aisle five."

"Thanks." Skirting around the salesman, he sprinted forward, the wheels on the cart almost leaving skid marks.

As he rounded the corner into the aisle his leg struck some shelving. The pain started up again. But he wasn't going to let it hold him back from his mission. Within seconds he whizzing down the narrow passageway lined with cans of weed killers, insecticides, and other chemical weapons designed for gardeners and home-owners intent on sterilising the environment. He scanned the rows of cans, jars, and cardboard boxes, inhaling the heady, acrid fumes that leached into the air around the display. It took him no time at all to spy the distinctive blue and white spray. He grabbed the jumbo size. 'Spider Grenade', it proclaimed in bold letters.

A doubt was starting to intrude as he studied the can. 'Perfectly safe,' the can reassured him, '...when used as directed,' it qualified. 'Guaranteed to kill spiders. Will not affect plants or mammals. Not recommended for use by children without adult supervision.'

He read no farther. He would just spray the stuff around the house and that would be the end of spiders, especially last night's unwanted visitor!

He had seen an advertisement on television that featured this very product. He had watched it was professional interest. He remembered how the actor had eyed the camera with a wide smile on his face. "This new chemical compound is designed to attach itself to the 'docking points' of protein in a spider's body," he had said, the camera cutting away to a computer graphic of what purported to be spider protein. "Once there," he continued in a voice overlay, "it stimulates an abnormal release of growth hormone that causes the arachnids to literally explode by growing faster than their exoskeleton is able to expand."

The camera cut back to the actor who was now passing through a spotless living room. "Within hours your house will be rid of the pests that have plagued mankind since we first set up house in caves. As for safety," the actor continued with a gleam in his eye, "You could use it like a breath freshener if you had to: though we don't recommend it for such use." The godlike being on the TV screen picked up the can, shut his eyes, and gave his face two good bursts of 'Spider Grenade'. Thirty-two capped teeth beamed at the camera. "Nice, minty taste, too!"

Sebastian came back to earth: he became aware of the girl at the checkout with her arm extended towards him. "Yes, did you want to buy that?" He paid and left.

Driving home he felt that things might be changing for the first time since he was five. He had been haunted for years by the memories and had never fully shaken the nightmares. Climbing into bed after evening prayers, settling down to sleep, feeling a pinprick on his ankle.

"Mum," he would call, suddenly wide-awake as a fiery pain climbed up his leg. The prick would occur a second time. "Mum!" he would scream, kicking his legs free of the blankets.

"What's wrong?"

"Something bit me," he would sob. "It's under the sheets."

"What, a spider you mean?" "How many legs does it have?" "Was it normal?" She would lift the covers and they would both peak cautiously under the sheet, just in time to see a tiny, hairy spider scampering away. The creature usually dropped over the corner of the bed, before his mother could squash it, and dart under the bedside table.

Since then he had feared the multi-legged monsters. No matter how many he smashed and sprayed, there were always more to take the place of their fallen comrades. But of course this was before the advent of 'Spider Grenade'!

Twenty minutes later he was parked in his driveway staring out at the house. It wasn't a big place: just one story, with five rooms and a bathroom. The giant tin he had purchased would be more than enough.

He cautiously crept into the house through the back door, as though he were trying to sneak up on the hoard of spiders that he knew were lurking in the dusty corners.

He had decided to let the pesticide off in the spare room next to the desk where the offending bug had appeared, but not before he had opened all inside doors and made sure that no windows were left open.

At last, he was all set up. He popped off the lid and clutched the aerosol can in sweaty fingers, swallowing convulsively as he prepared for the assault. Taking a deep breath and holding it, he started a cloud of gas pouring upward into the room. He walked quickly through the house with his handkerchief clasped to his face, closed the outer door behind him and climbed into his car. He knew he would have to stay out of the house for three hours, as recommended on the can, but was content to sit it out in the padded comfort of his car seat. As he opened the car door it caught his leg. He winced and climbed in.

As time went on he found himself resting his head back against the headrest, his breathing became deeper...

-----ooo------

Sebastian was sitting down to a TV dinner, with all thought of the hectic events of the day behind him, when he first heard the news. The television was talking softly to itself, as it often did, when Sebastian pricked up his ears.

"The Environmental Protection Agency announced today that it has ordered a halt to the sale of all 'Spider Grenade'", the TV newsreader said.

Sebastian sat up in my chair, tapping up the volume with my remote control. "During the news conference," the announcer continued, "the spokesperson for the manufacturer maintained that the product has proven highly effective at killing spiders. Government sources at the EPA admitted that the product presented no environmental danger, but warned that strange reports resulting from its use needed to be investigated".

Sebastian got up and went through to his reading-room to check around his desk. No traces of the stuff remained, not even the strange odour that had taken lots of window opening to clear. There was no apparent sign that he had even debugged the place.

The clock chimed out as he crossed the small hallway. He didn't notice the extraordinary number of times it sounded. He entered the room slowly. He didn't know what he was looking for, or for that matter, why he was bothering to look at all! The news item hadn't been very specific. He stood for a moment scanning the room; the walls, the ceiling, the floor, the desk. The desk! It had something on it that shouldn't be there! A thread of web hung bright and thick from the rim of his beautiful lamp. The lamp had been turned on and it was vibrating, giving off a low humming sound. The glistening twine was gently swaying to the reverberation of the lamp. He had cleaned the whole place thoroughly, especially his lamp. This just wasn't possible!

"What in the world is going on here?" he asked himself.

As he approached the desk the humming grew louder. It was an eerie buzzing noise that was somehow voice-like. Like someone making a deep throaty noise before speaking. Something began to drag at his shoes. He looked down and saw a network of sticky ropes that glistened as if covered with wet glue. A movement from the far corner of the room caught his eye. Struggling to maintain his balance, he twisted around, peering into the dark corner while grasping the side of the desk. The ceiling light glinted off five large rubies that sparkled in mid-air. It took a few seconds for Sebastian to realise what I was looking at. His jaw went slack as the creature moved a little further into the light.

Whether Sebastian liked it or not, he was standing face-to-face with a spider that stood as tall as a man! It had a body the size of a large pumpkin, with long, hairy legs that dropped straight to the floor.

He screwed his eyes shut, turned around awkwardly despite the tenderness in his leg, and dragging his feet through the slime, moved towards the door in slow motion. Somehow he plucked up the courage to look back over his shoulder. The thing stood motionless, its fangs glistening in the light from the cobweb-covered electric light bulb.

Something inside Sebastian snapped. He screamed. Then he screamed some more. He stood in the doorway with his back to the horror and screamed.

"Take it easy," a voice said. "You're not in any danger. I am only here to help. I am so pleased I managed to get through. It didn't work the first time."

"What?" the man asked. "Who's there? You've got to help me."

"Just as well you have a strong heart. I didn't realise how personally fearful of spiders you were. But there's no reason to be so afraid. Please be calm."

"What?" his eyes focusing with disbelief on the beast across the room. "How can you be talking to me? I must be mad!"

"No, no, you're not mad," the spider seemed to say to him. It rubbed its two front legs across its hairy head and then continued. "I'm not really talking you know, not as such. After all I don't have the proper mouthparts for that. You see, there is this thing called the 'articulatory base', it varies from language to language, but it's basically the 'standby position' automatically adopted by a creature's speech organs when they prepare to speak, and is peculiar to their native language. I don't have an 'articulatory base' as such, but then, you're probably not interested in all that".

Sebastian didn't answer.

"Oh dear! How awkward! Well, I'll try to explain. Apparently this whole thing started when a rogue member of our race slipped through the space web, landed on a cheese-grater, barely escaped with his life but lost a leg in the process. Through some strange means that we have never been able to figure out this episode was 'transmitted' to the boy in the next room who immediately set about drawing the event with coloured crayons. A copy of this turned up a couple of years later in a book about superstitions of the twentieth century, and the rest is history. In a manner of speaking, that is.

"Ah! The seven-legged spider thing..." whispered Sebastian. The creature hardly noticed that Sebastian had spoken. In fact, it seemed to be quite enjoying itself.

"No," it continued, "what I'm doing is something along the lines of what you call telepathy. It works through the part of your brain that normally hears, so you perceive that my words are coming through your ears. Only of course they aren't."

Sebastian stood listening, trying to take it all in.

"No, you're not stark raving mad."

"But if I was," Sebastian reflected aloud in a dreamlike fashion, "if I was you'd seem to be saying just that. You probably aren't even there…"

"Tell you what," the spider interrupted. "If you're mad it doesn't really make much difference if we carry on with this conversation or not, does it?"

Sebastian pondered the logic of what was said. "Well, I suppose not."

"Good. My name is Pyglo"

"A spider with a name?"

"Of course! Now just listen for a bit and see if I make any sense. Reading your mind, I know that you've been trying to picture how much a spider like me would need to eat to stay alive. But, please don't be alarmed. After all, you wouldn't eat a fellow man, or any animal like a dolphin, if there was an outside chance that it was a sentient being like you, right?"

"That's true," he agreed cautiously.

"Well, this is true of my race as well. We eat only animals that are like the beasts you call cows. We never eat animals capable of using tools".

Sebastian shivered.

"Which is where you come in," Pyglo continued. "I see my visit here as a golden opportunity to put a proposition to you.

I'm sure our elders would agree that we'd like to carry on trade with your people. We could use the livestock you raise. Many of your farmers are looking for new markets and we need..."

Sebastian's thoughts were spinning out of control. Through the chaos of his thinking process, he found himself asking whether he was actually setting the groundwork for an intergalactic Trade Agreement with an alien bug resembling something out of a science fiction horror movie!

"Wait a minute, what do you mean by 'race'? You're part of a race of spiders?"

Pyglo was silent for a moment. "I'm sorry, I seem to be getting ahead of myself. Let me put it this way. The spiders on your planet are tiny little beasts with brains too small for little more than reflexive actions. It's only with the advent of the new hormones in the spray you used that they became large enough to support a nervous system capable of..."

"That spray was designed to kill spiders. No offence meant." Sebastian bit his lip.

"None taken. Yes, the aim was to kill spiders, but although some of your miniature creatures were indeed blown up, others went through an unexpected hormonal transformation. This resulted in the creation of some very large specimens that we mistook for members of our race that had somehow slipped through the space web into your world. We had an ongoing rescue programme running for several months before we realised our error. We knew something was wrong when they began arriving without being rescued!"

Sebastian was still having trouble looking at the thing. He struggled with his feet to turn around a little more. "You mean going from our world to yours?"

"Yes. They were arriving uninvited, as it were. Again, the pesticide you see. Once they were that large, they were smart enough to weave the web of travel, a pattern that warps space and allows my kind to trek from one world to another. That's how we discovered your orb and how am able to travel here. From the reports given by spiders coming across we learnt about the poison being used, and from the subsequent tests that were conducted we were able to deduce that some genetic tampering had taken place. It was clear that their genetic structure made their size impossible without hormonal modification, and this was indicative of a sophisticated civilisation. So it was my job to come here and, if I found such a culture, study it. I've actually been here for a couple of weeks reading your mind, learning all I could."

"I have seen your world, I think you should see mine."

Sebastian shuddered. He felt a chill run through his body.

Pyglo observed the reaction. "It'll be alright", he said in a comforting voice, as he moved across the room. "There needs to be some initial trust you know."

Sebastian squeezed his eyes shut and stood frozen. His racing thoughts were now slowing down and gradually sliding into blackness.

The great spider reached forward and pulled a netlike web around Sebastian. Once encased, the spider slung his guest over its back, much like a person would swing a duffel bag across their shoulder. The creature held the cargo securely with its two front legs. Sebastian writhed around to make his sore leg more comfortable.

"Don't fret, I'm not going to hurt you and we won't be gone long. Just relax and enjoy the ride."

Pyglo strode toward the dark corner, and entered a funnel in the web at breakneck speed.

Inside the swaying cocoon Sebastian wriggled around to make his leg more comfortable, then lost consciousness.

-----ooo------

Sebastian cautiously opened one eye and gasped at the shimmering rainbows in the web that surrounded him.

"The glowing streams of light beyond the web are stars," the hairy creature below him explained. "We're travelling at hyper-light speeds. My planetary system is right there, in front of us."

Abruptly they swung to one side and dived down a fork in the tunnel. Moments later they arrived in Pyglo's world with its green sky and two pink suns overhead.

Sebastian gazed through the webbing at the ground, which was covered with white silk that looked like snow. Webs formed mounds with gaping doorways and some of the structures stretched upward, vanishing into the fluffy clouds above. Vast numbers of 'Pyglo's scampered to and fro, ignoring the human in the same way that somebody on a busy street back home might ignore a stranger.

"They don't seem to see me", Sebastian commented.

"They don't see you, I have 'cloaked' you for this visit."

"As you can see, we are very peaceful here," Pyglo said, motioning with one leg. "Now, let me set you free. But don't stray far, it would be easy to get lost and right now

I'm the only one who knows the exact return route to your reading-room."

"Don't worry, I don't intend to wonder off!"

The spider touched the webs and the net fell free.

"How did you do that?"

"It's a bit complicated. Sure you want to know?"

Sebastian sighed and shook his head.

"You'll find that we have advanced way beyond the spiders you have on earth, just like you've advanced beyond the monkey's of your planet. Brains make all the difference, you know."

The human space-traveller took in the sights. The place was beautiful in its own way. He had a thousand questions he could ask. Too many! He turned to his fellow time-traveller, who in some strange and incomprehensible way was becoming easier to look at. "OK. We are here. Now tell me why you have brought me here? What is it that you want with me? Why me in particular, I mean?"

"It's simple really. We have no skills at raising animals. But we're experts at generating all types of strong building materials, from woven silk cloth to thick, durable cables. These materials are all much stronger than steel and only one-hundredth of its weight. We can create our silk according to specification, made to order and delivered to a buyer's doorstep. Using the mode of travel that you have just experienced first hand. My studies of your planet tell me this material would be very valuable to your clothing industries."

Sebastian knelt down and swept up a handful of the silky stuff that covered the ground. He inspected it carefully. "Could resins be added to this stuff," he asked.

"A very astute question I must say. I knew I had picked wisely when I proposed you to the Council of Elders. Yes. In fact, with the addition of resins, our silk is suitable for the construction of super-strong and super-light sheaths for buildings, cars, and aircraft. Several of our trading partners are even using it for building their spacecraft."

"But where do I fit in?" Sebastian asked. "Why not simply go direct to the United Nations and…"

Pyglo raised a leg by way of interjection. "The fact is most of your people hate spiders. We have what your kind calls a 'public-relations problem' of the worst kind."

Sebastian could not deny the fact. Although it was only a matter of perception, throughout the human race it was a perception of the strongest kind. He smiled apologetically and nodded.

"We have had to deal with this problem before, with other worlds. The last thing the majority of your people would want to deal with is a bunch of eight-legged monsters. Spiders are associated with all manner of evil on your planet. So, first your people must be educated so they can understand that we are a good race and mean them no harm. Only then can the market for our products be fully exploited."

Somewhere in Sebastian's brain a light went on. "You mean an advertising campaign! Yes, of course, you want me to produce a campaign that changes our perceptions about you and your race."

"Exactly. I've followed your advertising expertise and know you are the one for the job."

The adman had a glazed look. His inventiveness had kicked in. Under his breath he started to develop a strategy.

"We'll need to start subtly. I'll hire a few freelancers to write science articles about how beneficial spiders are. I'll arrange to publish speculative pieces here and there about how alien cultures could mean big markets for Earth's products. Then we'll need to go to children's literature. Get them used to the idea of thinking pro-spider."

"How big of a hurry are you in?" He was obviously warming to the prospect of writing and running the biggest advertising campaign in human history.

"You can take as long as you like. The main thing is to get it right. We need this huge market to remain open to us, and of course we will support you while you while you work for us. I'll be your direct contact and use the same signal as before, with the same means of communication. It'll be good working with you Sebastian. Highly rewarding for both of us. Some of our other customers trade gold for our silk and I understand gold is valuable on your world, although we have found little use for it in our culture."

The enormity of what Sebastian was about to get into was making him giddy. With a burst of childish energy, he went running through the silky ground-cover kicking it from side to side as he ran, like a boy tramping through a field of newly mown hay. He had almost forgotten the troublesome leg.

His elation was cut short by a stumble, which sent him forward, face first. He wasn't hurt by the fall because of the cushioning effect of the softness of the ground, but for a moment his face was smothered. A faintness came over him. He felt a strange drifting sensation...

-----ooo------

Sebastian stirred. He had a headache. His return to consciousness was slow and full of strange images.

Visions were swirling round in his head. Ugly and bizarre visions, all seemingly unconnected. He saw images of some huge, hideous creature; enormous, white mountains, not white-capped, but white; rainbows of light, a gigantic, dark web in the corner of a room, a television newsreader and a brightly coloured spray can. None of these things made any sense at all. Just a jumble of unrelated odds and ends that had no meaning.

As he came out of his dreamlike state Sebastian was more than a little nervous about opening his eyes. Where was he? He had the idea that he might be lying on the ground, covered with threads of some kind. Then another notion entered his mind. He imagined that he was in a sack, being swept along and tossed around. Another thought swept over him, less worrying than the others. This gave him the impression that he was sitting in a car, waiting for something. His final impression, and one far more comforting, was that he had fallen asleep at his desk.

He opened his eyes. He was at his desk. His lovely desk! It had never looked and felt and smelt so good! He realised that he had never left it. He knew had just come out of the worst set of nightmares he had ever experienced. He felt sure he had not just been through one bad dream, but a whole series of them!

Sebastian showered the cold sweat from his body and prepared to turn in for the night. The steaming water generally improved the way he felt physically, but his leg was still tender, and he knew it would take time to eradicate the evil sensations that had wracked his brain. When he eventually climbed into bed he found that going off to sleep was not easy. The strange images wouldn't go away. Sebastian tossed around for hours before finally getting a short and unsettled sleep.

The next day at the office was no easier. Throughout the day he found it almost impossible to concentrate on his work, although by mid afternoon the memories and images from the previous day had faded away. Nevertheless, he was greatly relieved when the day was done and could hardly wait to return to the comfort and relaxation of home. He was tired and looking forward to catching up on a good night's sleep.

It was almost ten when Sebastian prepared for bed. He was making a glass of warm milk in the kitchen when he first noticed the vibration. It was a familiar resonance, but he couldn't quite place it. As he neared his reading room a powerful fear gripped him. It all came flooding back again. Surely, this couldn't be happening! There had to be some simple explanation for the noise. As he entered the reading room the clock struck thirteen.

His lamp was dancing on the desk!

"Pyglo calling Sebastian, Pyglo calling Sebastian. Come in please…"

-----ooo------

Robert snorted and turned over. The alarm kept going. He lazily raised an arm and dropped it on the clock. It hit the button and silence fell on the room. Jane stirred and murmured, "Good morning". He moaned back.

"You OK?" she asked.

"Do we know anybody called Sebastian?" he asked.

"No. I don't think so. Why do you ask?"

"Oh. Nothing, just a silly dream really."

She turned to face him. "How's your leg?"

He flexed his leg beneath the covers and groaned. "Sore. I don't think I slept very well."

"I don't know why you keep playing cricket", she chided softly, "after all, you've had so many injuries. I reckon it's a dangerous game!"

He wiggled his leg again and looked beneath the blanket. A pungent odour rose up from the warmth of the bed. "It does feel a bit better. I think the cream helped."

"Phew! I should think so, considering how much guck you slapped on!" She smiled and made a big show of fanning her face.

He dropped the blanket and watched her flapping hand. She had been very patient about it all. "You're right, I've being thinking of quitting anyway. That'll be my last game."

"I'll put the kettle on," she said in a comical voice, holding her nose. Jane sprung out of bed and hurried to the kitchen.

She had never liked the smell of camphor!

It Really Must

It's very quick, the sound of a tick.
It's very slick, like that of a click.
Not like a lick, more like a kick'
     Is the sound of a tick.

Awfully lush, is the sound of the slush.
It's certainly plush to hear it mush.
     It isn't a hush, nor a crush.
          Just slush.

I'd always choose to hear it ooze.
For when it woos peoples shoes,
A summer cruise you'd even loose,
     To hear it ooze.

But to really blend, it has to end.
No good to send it round a bend
In order to wend its way to mend.
     It really must end.

Dawn

Morning, twiggy, twilight hours.
Clipping through the village lanes
These heels do a rhyme make.
And oft before any bird dreams it time
To lead his friends, in earl morning chime.

Hedgerow smells sweet.
Listen..., even now the drops of golden morning
Fall through leaves, dark and green.
They soak the roots to keep firm these soft walls
For day-time feet to go between.

Quietitude, soft morning sky, streaks of heaven.
A feeling of, well, awe.
Yet something else.
That sense of sharing a mostly hidden wonder,
At a time when others sleep.

Ah, morning's coming, my heels are slowing,
The light is growing.
The hedge drops going.
Yes. Yes there it went.
The night is spent.
A new day sent...
There went the first cheep.

Close Call

A woman was slowly stroking the back of his hand as he came to his senses. Gradually his vision cleared and he saw her, the smile on her face, the nodding head.

"You're okay, Mr. Smith, you've been involved in an accident. Just try to relax now."

He could hear himself thinking. 'Accident'. There seemed to be a voice repeating itself in his head. The woman sounded out there somewhere, the echo of her voice hollow and distant, yet she was right next to him, right by his side, holding his hand. Was there any pain? He tried to feel for pain but only felt numbness. Was he paralysed?

"You're fine, Mr. Smith, we've just given you a little something to help you relax, okay? You might feel a little panicky, and you may not be able to feel your legs, but everything is as it should be. Do you understand?"

It wasn't exactly reassuring but he nodded. Try as he might he could not feel any sensation in his legs. He could feel his hand resting in hers, so why no feeling in his legs? He tried to remain calm. The woman had told me him everything was okay, no need to panic, just keep calm, but his head started to swim.

"Mr. Smith… Mr. Smith," she repeated, we have someone who wants to ask you a few questions, do you feel up to it?"

The man in the bed felt afraid, numb, cold, and yet he was happy to answer questions on the grounds that it just might take his mind off the thought that he could feel nothing below his waist.

"Yes. OK. I think I'm okay. Tell me… I am okay aren't I?"

"Of course you are, just relax, I'll be right here, Mr. Smith." She smiled, opened the curtain a little, and beckoned to the waiting man. He gripped her hand even tighter. She looked down and smiled, as she patted his hand.

"Hello Mr. Smith, I'm sorry to see you this way, but I do have to ask you a few questions, the nurse tells me you're doing okay, out of danger. That's good."

"Really, thank you, that is good to hear. I can't feel my legs, did you know that?"

The nurse chimed in.

"You will, Mr. Smith, I promise you, perhaps a few minutes that's all, then your legs will be fine. Please relax and just answer the policeman's questions."

Policeman? He never thought, didn't understand, didn't realise, until she actually said that. He looked at his uniform, his cap under his arm, and a notebook in his hand. Yes, white shirt and black tie, smart, official, authoritative. He felt his stomach turn over.

"Now then, do you remember anything of the accident, Mr. Smith?" he said, looking down at his notebook, his pencil poised.

"No, sir, I don't."

"Do you recall leaving home at all?"

He was so conscious of no feeling in his lower body he could hardly think straight at all.

"No, I'm afraid I don't."

"You do know who you are, correct?"

"Yes. Malcolm Smith."

"And your address, sir?"

"Number 11, Krisp Street. That's Krisp with a'"

The policeman smiled. "Being as you live there, that would be a Smith's Krisp then sir?"

The woman tensed and glared at the officer. The policeman coughed and suddenly became very awkward. He shuffled his boots in order to composed himself. "Begging your pardon sir. Now, to the matter at hand."

The policeman leaned forward and lowered his voice. He was now deadly serious.

"Mr. Smith, I do have to tell you some sad news I'm afraid. This is necessary for me to complete my inquiries you understand. The car you were driving…well, it mounted a pavement. I'm afraid there have been fatalities."

Fatalities? The man in the bed was beginning to lose any sense of sanity. This was all so unreal! First his legs, or the lack of them; then his memory going, with no idea how he got to where he was. His being questioned by a policeman; jokes about the name of his street, and now, apparently, people have been killed!

Tears welled up in his eyes. "For God's sake. What fatalities?"

"Yes, well, a mother and a child were killed today, and two others were injured and admitted to this same hospital."

His head was pounding. A deafening pulse filled his ears. His body became cold and a feeling of overwhelming nausea racked his body.

His eyes rolled and the nurse came forward.

"Mr. Smith... Mr. Smith... It's okay, gently now... gently... you're okay" Again, he could feel her hand gripping his. He held onto it tightly. "Try to relax your body, Mr. Smith, you're having a hard time breathing. In.... out... in... and out... keep in time with me please. A bigger breath this time, and in...now out... and again...in... and out, that's better, keep that going."

The nurse called the policeman back. "You can continue now." She squeezed his hand reassuringly.

"You don't recall using your mobile phone at any time, Mr. Smith?" He felt a drift of guilt at the question. He did his best to recall. He tried to picture himself at the wheel, to see the phone. There was no memory of it.

"No, sir, I do not recall anything. A mobile phone you say?"

"Yes. You do own one I take it sir?"

"Yes. Yes, I do. But…"

"Eye witnesses at the scene say you were seen driving while using a phone. You definitely don't recall this?"

There was something in the policeman's voice that said he was not happy with the man's statements. A mother and a child were dead. The man in the bed suddenly felt very afraid, and very alone. He was alive, yet a mother and child were dead; dead because he was apparently using a mobile phone while driving. How could any of this have happened? How could this have happened to him without any sense of it being real? Was he blocking out reality because it was all too horrible to face up to?

His glazed eyes stared up at the ceiling. He had vivid pictures of people innocently standing, walking, and playing, when his car had smashed into them. Just one thoughtless act. A stupid phone call. A call to whom, and why; what could be so important that he would risk creating such havoc and death? He had no answers, nothing made sense, and his mind began slowly slipping away...

"Do you have a reading there, nurse?"

It was a distant question, echoing in some far off place.

"Yes, Mr. Granger, it's a good reading. I think we are all done here. You said you wanted to get off sharp today."

The nurse helped the policeman off with his jacket. He bent over the apparatus.

"Let me see now. Ah! A good result, yes." The Policeman, now in shirtsleeves, tore the paper off the machine. "I'll sign him off and if you don't mind. Sorry about the 'Krisp' thing."

She lowered her head. "I was *so* embarrassed."

The man in the bed stirred. Feeling was flooding into his legs now. His head was clearing, and he could hear sounds: perfect sounds, no echo, not sense of the noise being a long way off.

"Ah! Feeling better are we? I said you would be all right". She peeled back the covers. "Can you swing your legs off the bed, Mr. Smith?"

He could now hear traffic, and people talking just beyond the door.

"You'll be remembering why you came now, Mr. Smith," she said, busily signing off his papers at a desk.

He stood by the bed, looking round, still feeling rather feeble.

"Don't worry, you now have a full driving licence. You passed the simulated accident scenario. Your guilt level was *excellent*."

She held out a piece of paper.

"Just hand this to the registrar when you leave. If you still feel a little unsteady there is a waiting room down the hall where you can get a nice cup of tea and a biscuit."

As he handed the paper to the registrar, memories from earlier in the day flooded back. One of his colleagues yelling good luck as he left the office; his fiancé driving him to the centre. She had been so confident that he would pass, she had left the car for him and returned to her own office by bus.

Suddenly, he felt a hand tap his shoulder.

"Well done." The phoney policeman was passing on his way out. "I must say, your 'guilt' response was exceptional. Just remember, okay, no using the phone while you're driving."

"No! No! Indeed not" he replied, taking the slip of paper that made it legal for him to drive away without supervision.

He started to feel a lot better after the ordeal. He found the car and moved away quickly with confidence and more than a little pride.

His mobile sounded. He pulled it from his pocket.

"Hello..."

Summer Hot

Hot and sticky, sweaty summer,
Brought to frizzle dog and man.
Dusty, drying, burnt and frying,
Take cooling shadow if you can.

Squelchy mushiness, snowbound things,
Are hopeful visions, seen by those
Who thirst and groan, and drag their legs,
And snap, finally, go their withered bones.

Hot and sticky, sweaty summer,
Choking, croaking, peeling sun.
Hang your heat and damn your glow,
And miss you much when winter comes.

Duskiness

Now is the time when dusky light
Mixes with beams of artificial glare,
And blending tones from peoples' homes
Sift through blue-grey squares.

Now, in sombre softness,
The shadows merge and interplay.
Trees appear an ashy grey.
Black buildings stand,
Dark yet grand.
Monuments to yet another span.
Another dead day.

A Nursery Story

A tiny spider rested on the page of an open book. It of course had no idea that it was about to be disturbed, or that its movement across the page would have anyway significance in the whole scheme of things. The book was old and faded but had been very special to a young boy who had once lived in the house, and at a time when it had been a nursery.. The room was now abandoned. It had been closed up on the last day of the trial. An episode that had irreversibly changed the lives of those who once inhabited what was now a derelict farmhouse. Soon after the room was shut the property itself was abandoned.

The boy who had occupied the room as a child grew up and eventually inherited the family farm. He married a local girl. They had produced one child, a daughter. He was never really meant to be a man to work the land and had let it run down. As the years went by the livestock were not replaced, the buildings were allowed to rot, and very little in the way of farming was done at all.

Now, as it happened the extensive acreage that went with the farm meant that he could make a reasonable living by simply mowing all of the meadows and stacking the grass after it had dried. He established himself as the main supplier of hay within the immediate district and beyond. His venture boomed when a partnership was formed with a local businessman to use his trucks to deliver his fodder far and wide.

All went well for several years until the farmer discovered that the trucking business was making extra profit by understating the amount of product being delivered and pocketing the extra income. He found by looking back through the records that two very large orders had been the main source of extra revenue for the transport company. The farmer visited his associate one evening with the intention of having it out with him. He felt badly done by and a terrible argument took place. The meeting ended with a dreadful fight taking place in the trucker's garage. A large spanner was picked up. There was a vicious blow to the head and the business owner lay dead.

What followed has already been alluded to. The farmer's wife closed the door of what had been there daughter's bedroom on the day of the execution. It was still full of old toys and books once owned by her late partner. Items left there from a time when the room was his. The girl didn't fully understand why she had to move into her mother's room for those last few days. Like most children she loved her room and found solace and comfort in its familiarity. What she did understand was that being diddled twice in business deals did not justify beating a man to death. For the woman, she realised that the prospect of selling the place was poor because of its condition. Despite the fact that the property was likely to remain something of a white elephant a short time after these horrible events the mother and daughter left the district determined to start a new life.

The woman had an uncle who owned a boat-building yard she had not seen for several years. He had often asked her to visit. Naturally, he was familiar with the case from the reports given in the papers and was more than happy to take them in. They were given board above one of the main workshops and soon settled down. The girl was now in her teens and started at a local school to finish her education. She had developed a keen interest in astronomy from childhood and was thrilled to find that the school had a special programme in place that was being sponsored by a space exploration company.

Meanwhile, the benevolent uncle was becoming very wealthy by building large, luxury catamarans for those who could afford them. His business was booming and he wouldn't accept anything more that very small rent for the rooms made available to his relatives. For the next three years mother and child enjoyed a relatively trouble free existence before the next event changed the course of their lives yet again.

The boat-builder continued to thrive and his company's assets seemed to grow by the minute. In fact, he was making so much money that it generated a high degree of interest, and not a small measure of curiosity, within the offices of the income tax authorities. So much so that unseen investigations went on for a number of months before officers swooped and removed all his books. They spent several more weeks combing through bank statements and the like before bringing changes against him for tax evasion. It became apparent that he had been, to put it bluntly, fiddling the books. The main charge involved one particularly large and luxurious boat and the concealment of such large sums of money that the man's firm went into liquidation and the tenants in the upstairs rooms had to move out.

Now, it happens that during the time she had been on the space research programme through the school, the daughter had done particularly well. It seemed that she could apply for work in the company's main research lab in another town and under the circumstances the move would suit them both. All went well and within a few short days they had moved their belongings into lodgings not far from the girl's new place of work. At this point the farm was still on the market but had not attracted any interest.

As it turned out the school-leaver had joined the organisation at an exciting time. They were due to send up an unmanned research craft that had been designed to make a lunar landing. It was programmed to land on the surface where it would sit for several months sending back data about the moon's environment and details of its weather patterns. In the first weeks of joining the team the girl visited the site where the craft was being prepared for the launch.

Although most of her work involved helping to type up schedules for various lunar experiments, she had the opportunity to spend time in the physical presence of the ship. Despite it not being built to accommodate a crew it was still a formidable size. The large girth of the ship, together with the fact that it had two adjacent antennas near the cone, gave rise to it being rather unkindly referred to as 'the cow' by the technicians preparing it for its flight. Despite any frivolity from the workers they all knew that the mission was a very important stage in the life of the company and all hopes were being pinned on its success. Several backers had invested time and money in the project and no real benefits would be reaped until the mission's results were beamed back to Earth.

A few months later, humour gave way to gloom when the craft left its planned trajectory and sailed on past its lunar target, only to disappear into deep space. This was technically known as a 'jump over'. The impact it had on the company was financially crippling and on the young worker less obvious. She decided with her mother's agreement that she should move to a nearby city and try to go it alone. Considering the traumas that her daughter had been through the mother supported her attempt at making a better life for herself.

With her science qualifications and short-term exposure to the space project she eventually found a position with an animal research institute. She soon settled into what she considered to be quite fascinating work. Her main duties involved documenting and recording test results. The institute had made some major advances in the field of stimulus-response mechanisms in animals. There subjects, mainly dogs, were being subject to visual stimulation as opposed to the traditional techniques based on sound.

At the same time it should be stated that the company of a young man who worked in an office close to where she regularly sat taking notes made the work even more pleasurable. They were soon spending time together after work. They seemed to share a number of interests. He was very keen on visiting the local museum as often as he could and she was happy to accompany him. He seemed to have some very grand ideas about what he would do with his life, but she was content to let him dream.

Back in the laboratory their best dog subject, this happened to be a Chihuahua, was showing remarkable gains when being stimulated visually by running videos of tennis matches. The animal seemed to become excited when volleys were taking place. But the most ground-breaking results were when the research team captured several seconds of video of what they thought was joviality expressed in short sharp giggles. Much debate was had about what this actually meant and there was a general air of excitement around the building.

Meanwhile the young man's passion for visiting the museum hit its height with the news that a major collection was being displayed over the coming weekend. Plans were made to meet at the museum as the doors opened to allow the maximum viewing time. Although the thought of spending a whole Saturday at a museum was not the girl's idea of a good time, she went along on the back of the young man's enthusiasm. The weather had turned really cold and at least they would be in a warm building. She had been having some niggling doubts about their relationship. After all, on reflection, her initial attraction to him was based on flattery. In fact she felt quite embarrassed when she thought about how he had won her over by telling her that she was a 'real dish'. As it transpired, these doubts were about to come to an abrupt end.

They met as arranged and entered with the early crowd. The exhibition was very popular. It was made up mainly of small, valuable pieces from the private collection of an Indian Maharaja. He had allowed a number of museums around the country to run the displays, rotating from town to town. Many of the items were made of gold, silver, or ivory, and most of it was lavishly encrusted with precious jewels. There were combs, hairclips, and broaches in one glass display case, smoking pipes, cigarette cases, and tobacco tins in another. Beautiful garments were hung in tall glass-fronted cabinets and the largest section of the exhibition was given over to a display of magnificent dinner-sets and cooking utensils. There were cups, chalices, cutlery sets, and decanters, all made from precious metals and all individually crafted and presented to the owner. The centrepiece of this display was a huge diamond encrusted tablespoon made of solid gold. It was all very precious, and in the main irreplaceable. As a consequence of this the security in the building had been visibly beefed up since their earlier visits.

The incident that put an end to any doubts the girl had about her friend took no more than a minute to play out. It was nearly midday when the alarm bells went off. As she turned to look for her companion he ran into her full pelt almost knocking her to the ground and with a wild look ushered her out of the building. She knew something was wrong but could hardly believe that he was the cause of the chaotic scenes they left behind. He dragged her across the road, telling her everything was alright and he would call round to see her the next day. She watched as he disappeared through the park they had often visited on their lunch breaks. The weather seemed even more bitter now. She pulled her duffle coat tighter and walked into the park, leaving the sound of bells and people shouting. Arriving at the seat they had often used, she sat down quietly for a while, and then cried. She put the hood of her coat over her head and cried for the best part of an hour before moving on.

Something deep inside took hold of her as she sauntered back to her lodgings. Would she go back to her mother? Would she just move on and try another town, another job? Or would she disappear off the face of the planet, as so many people had managed to do. She had seen television programmes about those who go missing deliberately. That was what she would most like to do. She needed time to think; time to reflect. She needed somewhere safe, quiet, where she could be alone for a while. A place where she could just think. As she arrived at her rooms the solution came to her. With a great burst of enthusiasm two suitcases were roughly packed, cash was counted, and a dash to the central bus station all took only a few minutes. She was going home.

She arrived in the late afternoon and conserved her finances by walking from the town out to the farm. She prayed that it had never been sold. Entering the property she could see that it stood empty. She thrilled at the thought of entering her room. Her special place and resting up for a while. That was all she needed. Just a place to rest, and to think, and to plan. She reflected on the idea that everybody needs that at some time in their life.

None of the furniture had been removed from the house, and the back window was still the best place to get in if you didn't have a key. The power had been turned off long ago but she knew where the emergency candles had been tucked away. She wasn't at all hungry although she still had sandwiches she had bought at the bus-station. She would think about food and water tomorrow. She would think about all sorts of practicalities tomorrow. In the meantime she would sit, and think, and sleep in her own room.

She pushed the door open and entered. It smelt a little musty and was rather dull looking by the yellow flame of the candle, but it was beautiful. It exactly was what she wanted, what she needed. She went back down by candle light and brought up her cases. She laid them on the bed and started to pull out badly creased clothing. She didn't see the object wrapped in one of the museum's towels from the gents' toilets. She hadn't notice it fall from her duffle coat pocket at her lodgings as she gathered up her belongings. She had paused for a brief moment at the time when packing her cases, but threw it in anyway. Other considerations were much more important to her then. Anyway, she did not notice it now as it rolled off the back of the bed. The gentle thud that it made as it passed through the broken floor board was swamped by the noise of clothes being shaken straight. The recovery of the Maharaja's property was not likely to occur in the near future.

After covering the windows so that the world outside wasn't aware of her sanctuary, and setting two candles up near her bed, she sat down at her little desk. A tiny spider scampered across the page of an open book. She sat, staring down at the fading pictures of animals. It brought back a flood of happy memories. As she stared at the lines beneath the pictures they seemed to come to life. The words took on a vivid appearance, seemingly lifting from the paper. With no idea of how especially meaningful the words were, she read softly to herself…

Hey, diddle, diddle,
The cat and the fiddle,
The cow jumped over the moon.
The little dog laughed
To see such sport,
And the dish ran away with the spoon.

The Silence From Within

Silences are manifold and all about abound.
The silence of a plastic spoon, rotting in the ground.
The silence of a mirror, hung in an empty room.
The silence of the dust that hangs
on the bristles of a broom.

The silence of the setting sun, inching out of view.
The silence of a white cloud's shape, swapping old for new.
The silence of a wall, that stands without a door.
The silence of grey ashes spread across a forest floor.

The silence of a poet, when his race is run.
The silence of a traitor, after the deed is done.
The silence of a breath that's held,
at the moment of a threat.
The silence of a back that's turned
when a plea will not be met.

But the silence most amazing, even silent when it speaks,
Is the silence that a mortal hears when self-awareness peaks;
When the sounds of thought and
notion and all the parts therein
Make way for warm tranquillity; the silence from within.

When a Muse Goes Missing

Writing poems is not always a breeze.
The muse can abscond with alarming ease.

When a muse falls silent and all ideas fly,
They leave a great hole... with no goodbye!

You can beg and cajole, but still she sleeps.
Your creative flair a prisoner she keeps.

Knowing I'm beaten I give up the fight,
And turn my back on the screen for the night.

I close my eyes with a forlorn sigh.
My head is empty and I wonder why.

Without a single idea in sight
I close the computer, and say goodnight.

But just as I lay drifting off to sleep,
Into my head bright notions creep.

So now I sit scratching in a quiet house.
No pc, no keyboard, no screen or mouse.

Finally, I return to my waiting bed
With words and phrases all gone from my head.

A short sleep leaves me drained and numb,
But this will pass in time to come.

My eyes are puffy; my back stiff as a board;
And all because... my muse had got bored!

Swing Time

It is spring time and a small boy lolls in his swing seat, dreamily staring out across the park. This is the first time he has been allowed to visit the park alone. He is shaded by the great oak that covers this part of the playground. The sun is warm on his legs with each forward motion out of the shade. Shouting and laughing of other children fills the air. The boy watches them from afar. He is not a mixer. He enjoys his own company; but as youngsters go, he is likeable enough.

It is summer; a young man is playing with a group of friends on the basketball court. Despite the heat of the day he dodges gracefully around the other players. He sends the ball high into the air and almost makes a basket. With the game over his attention turns to the lonely figure on the swings. The great oak was giving her shelter from the glare of the sun. She grinned as he approached. The young man sits down on the swing next to hers. She takes his sweaty hand in hers and together they sit in the peace of the advancing evening, swinging and watching the sun turn the sky to pale crimson.

It is now autumn in the park. A father sits on the swings, gently moving back and forth while watching his two children digging in the sand-box. He studies them intently, as they move sand from one corner to another; their faces are reddening from the cool air. An occasional breeze moves the leaves above him. Leaves float down from trees and settle across the green open field across the centre of the park. A great harvest moon shows against the blue. They run to him saying that their mother said not to be too late. They leave the park.

Winter has come to the park. An old man sits on a motionless swing, watching his labored breaths hang mistily in the cold air. The park is deserted. He watches smoke rising slowly from the chimneys of nearby homes. He sees the crooked basketball hoop against the evening sky. He stares at the sand-box. The old man slowly pulls himself off the swing and with tired limbs makes his way slowly to the sandbox. In the fading light, he stares into the darkening yellow and remembers. This would be his last time in the park. Tears form momentarily, but are wiped away quickly. A light snow begins to fall as the park slips away from him into total blackness.

The Humble Leveller

The judge sat high upon the case.
A scowling gesture on his face.
The charges would now move apace;
He didn't like the young man's race.

Now he too would have his say.
He would see the jury sway
And put the sorry fool away,
And damn his kind, come what may!

With wig and gown this lord was blessed,
While moral indignation gave him zest.
A prison term would seem the best,
Ignoring his attorney's quest.

The judge said "He must do his time,
The punishment must fit the crime".
The prisoner young, and in his prime,
Had failed to pay a parking fine.

The court officials, a callous bunch,
Just giggled at the judge's hunch.
While considering the credit crunch,
The judge said "I'll give him ten years after lunch".

The great man's sibling, full of mirth,
Yet free from prejudice since birth.
A moral girl, for what it's worth,
Contrived to bring him down to earth.

When all was quiet, the judges daughter,
Who knew her father didn't 'aughta,
Caused the eminent man to falter.
He froze as he reached his alter.
A toilet roll stood by his water!

The Coins of Nature

Precious things are seldom free,
But the coins of nature are there by decree.
They're scattered around where ever you go,
All put in motion a long time ago.

An arrow of birds in a stream of flight,
The fading of shadows in dying light,
Moonlight glinting on a rippling sea,
A myriad of greens on a single tree.

Dewdrops necklaced in a web,
The storm's echo as it starts to ebb,
The rattle of rain as it starts to pour,
A rumble of pebbles as they wash to shore.

The magic yellow of a new-born chick,
The crawl of a snail from brick to brick,
A wave of wind through a grassy field,
The scent of blooms on a waft revealed.

A bird's nodding head at a frantic feed,
The inapt beauty of an intruding weed,
A night owl's hoot from distant trees,
The smell of salt on an ocean breeze.

A stormy sky as clouds unfold,
The changing of colours as dusk takes hold,
The rustle of leaves on a balmy night,
A swirl of insects around a light.

A billow of leaves blown in a twist,
Sunlight glowing through a mist,
A sprinkling of stars in a crystal sky,
The flickering dance of a butterfly.

It's not too often that treasures are free.
It's not too often that all of us see.
Nature's coins are for all to share,
Regardless of who really put them there.

Time Again

The shop bell clanged as the old man stepped out onto the path to check the weather. Several children were playing in the street. He watched as the saucy kid from the big house on the corner wiggled his shiny new bike down the hill. The watcher smiled as he mounted the pavement and crashed into the newsagent's paper-stand across the road. It made a loud clatter as it hit the path, but no real damage was done. A loud squawk came from behind him. He turned back into his shop.

"Might get a customer or two. Never know your luck", he said to the parrot, which was now recovering from the disturbance. The bird looked up momentarily; then went back to its preening.

The antique shop had been there forever. The old man's grandfather first opened it so far back that no one in town would even know about it. Things had been slow. Things were always slow. His love of all the bits and bobs that surrounded him was all that kept him going year after year.

The shop didn't make any money; but he was contented enough. He lived from day to day on the bread line. He had never even been close to any real wealth. Not until now that is.

As usual, he was quite content to spend most of the morning fossicking about the poorly lit room, occasionally stopping to pick up some worthless object. This would be followed by a long period of admiration as he stared at it, as though he were holding some rare and priceless antique instead of a worthless piece of junk.

He stood gazing down at an old clock. It was the kind that had the workings visible through a glass dome. It sat on a wooden base. In all the years it had been in the shop it hadn't been moved. He decided to find somewhere for it at eye level and clean it up a bit. He stooped slowly to lift it. As his fingers felt around the base for the best grip something sprang out from the side. It was a drawer with something that had rattled as it opened. It contained a small, oddly decorated pocket watch.

"What's a watch doing inside a clock?" he mumbled. "My word! It is still ticking!" The old man moved closer to the window to get a better look. He glanced at the wall clock. To his amazement it was only two minutes fast! He reset the hands and instinctively rubbed it on his waistcoat.

At that moment there was a blinding flash that momentarily filled the shop. When he opened his eyes the shop owner was standing in total silence and blackness. The watch fell from his hand as he brought his hands up to his face. He rubbed his eyes and blinked as the light returned slowly, and with it the familiar sounds from the street. As he moved to peer into the street something crunched under foot. He bent and gathered up the broken pieces of the strange little watch. It was obviously beyond repair.

He was still reeling from his strange turn, and wondering whether it was down to the latest tablets he'd been taking, when the sound of something crashing outside grabbed his attention. His parrot squawked. As he walked through his front door he saw the boy dragging the paper-stand back in place and piling newspapers back where they belonged.

It took a while for the old timer to work out what had happened. He had wound the watch back by two minutes, and time itself had reversed with it! He looked down at the squashed case and tiny fragments of the timepiece, now spread out on the counter. He knew enough about old things to realise that it was beyond repair. It took him a little longer to appreciate that if this could happen for two minutes, why not several hours! He began to see the possibilities; the races, the lottery, the stock market! He now contemplated all that might have been; the riches, the travel, the possessions and the new life… His bird screeched again.

He looked up and smiled at his old friend. "Still, we might get a customer or two, eh?" he said, as he started fossicking again among the bits and bobs that surrounded him that kept him going year after year.

A Day in the Garden

When duty calls to chores in our grounds,
Just my gardening partner and me.
It's stretching the cliché to the limit, but…
It's really not my cup of tea.

As a school boy I read The English Garden,
An essay by Thackeray
In this, he counts the blessings it brings
My very first taste of quackery!

Each to their own, the saying goes,
But I don't see how this can be,
When there's stuff to pick up and bags to fill,
And it always falls to me.

There are weedings and scratchings and prunings and stuff,
In heaps, dotted here and there.
And as soon as a load is got out of the road,
On return, there's another one there!

There are grassy piles, thorny piles, leafy piles, twiggy piles;
One never knows what will appear.
There are high piles, low piles, long piles and short piles,
But nothing one could really hold dear.

And this goes on, to the dying sun
With my partner still hacking away.
And she hardly slows when I let her know
That we've both been at it all day.

Bags groan with the weight, as the ground get cleared,
With knees and back ever aching.
It's a wonderful sight, as day turns to night,
Of that, there is no mistaking.

To sum it all up, when you see it close-up,
It's a task that doesn't bring smiles.
And what it's about, without any doubt.
Is just miles and miles
Of scratches and trials
In short…just more bloody piles!

Poems

There are poems that say quite a lot
And those that say very little,
Others give guidelines for moving through life
While others are shy on committal.

Some read poems as a way of learning,
Some just need a good laugh.
Some struggle endlessly with hidden meaning
And never get past the first half.

While it's true that the verses can vary
And lines may hold secrets within.
At the end of the day, come what may,
One only gets out what goes in.

Poems don't always speak to us clearly,
Whether the poet knows it or not.
They may have had a really bad day
And just couldn't give a jot.

If you need to seek help with a line
You may reach out for some assistance,
So, in order not to waste your call
Remember, at all times; persistence!

A Courtyard View

"Enlightenment can be a thing of great beauty" the man said. "When natural science can become the norm and thrive in an environment where people let go of religion and dogma", he paused and fingered the book he held. He looked up at his visitor with a smile and went on. "When the authorities are seen to be working for the people and the people in turn start to think for themselves." He swung in his chair and looked out of the window.

He admired the spacious courtyard below and the fringe of green treetops in the distance for a few moments before turning back to the visiting professor.

"We, of course, are mostly concerned with physics. We both know that the whole thrust of physics is to discover truths about the nature of the physical universe, with nothing assumed or presupposed. Everything we see now and discover later has to be based on irrefutable evidence. It is true that occasionally our personal views or considerations may unduly influence our choice of a particular theory, but in the final analysis..." his voice dropped off as he studied the shapes of the shadows spreading across the great area below.

The visitor coughed softly to bring his friend back. "I agree, there is certainly a much greater uunderstanding of our work thanks largely to your brother..." The man bit his tongue as he realised what he had said. "I'm so sorry! I can't imagine what made me say that. I... I..."

The physicist raised his hand, "Don't apologise my old friend. He was a talented journalist with a very persuasive style of reporting. My brother is at peace now. The thing is done and that's that."

The visitor relaxed. "I'm sure you must be feeling a great sorrow...."

"Not at all! No; not a bit of it." replied the other. "Don't you bother yourself in that regard. As I said; he's at peace at last."

The men sat in complete silence for a while, until the visit was interrupted by approaching footsteps and a rattle of key at the door of the cell that announced the arrival of the priest, bible in hand, ready to administer the man his last rights.

Wherein Poetry Lies

We find it ever in our world,
Both in and out of sight,
Shadowed where no footsteps go,
Or dangling, burning bright.

We see it in an open flower;
Smell it, in driving rain.
We sit and dwell on past events
To bring it back again.

Poetry sounds in a rustling leaf
As well as a hacking cough.
It is born of life, of peace and strife
And none can turn it off.

It dwells within bark on an aging tree.
It shows in a baby's cry.
It floats on breezes, sweet or sour
And speaks as cars rush by.

It displays its lines in colour.
It forms in faint patterns of cloud.
It can dance in the eyes with shallow disguise
With no need to speak aloud.

It is found without sound in an old man's frown.
It can blossom from a dying bud.
Its refrain is the strain of a writer's toil;
With a silent pound in the blood.

The magic of music releases it.
It echoes in gloomy caves.
Dawn's mist and moonshine give it form
And it's heard in cresting waves.

And even in the heat of night
While thunder fills the skies,
We know where God has placed his hand,
And wherein poetry lies.

Of Knowing Where to Go

Should we be reasoning further?
Sifting through the clues.
Should we be pulling time apart?
Assuming we can choose.

Should we be looking with greater intent?
Seeking some ultimate proof;
With reality under the microscope;
Finding elusive truth.

Do each of us harbour some ancient awe,
With mystery locked in our souls,
That holds us fast from moving on,
That suspends the striving of goals?

Do we avoid time's strange ambiguity;
Each moment's the best place to start.
We need to see past the act of seeing;
To look without brain or heart.

Maybe our reason is lacking,
Or our faith to cross the abyss.
To recognise the worth of the search
And risk loss of immortal bliss.

Forever stands as a metaphor
For what we know as now,
And beyond the realm of what or why
Is the mystery of how.

We cannot see what we'd like to know.
It's more than our minds can plumb.
We get lost in the sense of some large intent,
And to lethargy we succumb.

Acceptance of both the nature and need
Of knowing where to go,
It seems a defeat, where these conflicts meet
To say that we shouldn't know!

A Mater of Moments

It took only a moment, in the blackness of the night, for the owl to swoop somewhat precariously through the blustering winds with uncanny silence; dipping suddenly with the intention of plucking an unsuspecting field mouse from the grassy tufts beside the farm gate.

---0---

At the same moment, the blackness made it hard going for the old vagrant making his way across the far side of the field, shortening his journey to the nearby town. It was only a small country town but he hoped that the night pickings would be good. The grocery store usually had scraps near the back door that had made this part of his round worth while in the past.

---0---

At that very same moment, in town, a boy stood eyeing the stuffed bird through the taxidermist's dirty window. The barn owl was perched on a branch, inside a glass-domed case at the back of the shop. The youngster loves owls. His mother comes out of the grocer's and crosses the road. "You're not looking at that old thing again, are you?"

The boy turned with the same look he had used a dozen times at least. "But, Mum. Look at it. It's beautiful!"

"Beautiful? It's an old stuffed bird! It probably smells."

"No. Look, it's in a glass case; it wouldn't smell, honestly. We could put it on Grandma's old table in the hall. That way we would see it every time we get home!"

The mother felt something stir from her own childhood. She smiled. "Come on. Let's see what your father has to say".

---O---

As the boy had stood staring in, in fact, at exactly the same moment, the man in the shop excused himself from his browsing customer and picked up the phone. His friend was calling about a boat trip they had planned. "I'm sorry" he was telling the caller, "I was looking forward to it too, but the winds are all over the place at the moment, very blustery, not at all predictable. The only predictable thing is the forecast; they say no change is expected for several days. That's the weekend out I'm afraid."

---O---

At the very moment the shop keeper had picked up the phone, a dustbin lid clattered to the ground across town, sending a cat scampering into the back yard. It hadn't been replaced properly and the wind had caught it. The cat retreated to its favourite safety spot up a tree at the end of the garden, where it could keep a watchful eye on things. It made its way there with an uncanny silence.

---O---

At the same time, in fact, at that exact same moment the phone was lifted, the boy who lived around the corner gave up on his homework. He slouched into the kitchen where his mother was preparing tea and sat with his face in his hands.

"What up?" she asks, surprised that he was not studying his favourite, and easiest to do, school subject.

"Computer's acting up again. I just lost some of my work".

"Oh no! That's rotten. Do you know what the trouble is?"

"Yeah. It's got to be the mouse..."

---O---

At the very moment the schoolboy had slammed his school book shut a man in a nearby house put his phone back on the receiver. He had taken the call while staring into his front garden. He now looked out with greater concentration and frowned at his lawn. The grass was in need of mowing. This was made more noticeable by the street light in front of the property. He called his son.

"Am I, or am I not, paying you pocket money to keep this tiny patch of grass looking good? Look at it!"

The boy looked half-heartedly at the front garden. "OK" he said reluctantly, "I'll do it weekend."

"I should think so; look, there are tufts of grass over there!"

---0---

In the same moment the father had put down the phone a gate slammed shut somewhere in the neighbourhood. An elderly woman struggled out of her armchair and made her way to the window. Satisfied that nothing was wrong she returned to her television. She enjoyed shows about the animal kingdom, and she found this week's programme on birds of prey of particular interest.

---0---

At the moment the gate had slammed, in a field just outside of town, in the blackness of the night, the owl that had swooped somewhat precariously through the blustering winds with uncanny silence; dipped suddenly and plucked an unsuspecting field mouse from the grassy tufts beside the farm gate, and disappeared with it into the night.

Summer Heat

There are those who don't long for summer,
They say they prefer the cold.
They would gladly move to cooler climes.
That's what I've been told.

They take no joy from the clicking of bugs,
Or the shimmering haze of the day,
Or kids gathering round an ice cream van,
Or mossies, with their aerial ballet.

They care nothing for the eucalypt scent,
Or the heat of a summer breeze,
Or the golden rays that last all day,
Or the drone of a thousand bees.

They can't abide a bright sapphire sky,
Or the warm damp of evening air,
Or the way the heat burns up through their shoes,
Or the sweat that runs down through their hair.

But for one who has come from a wintry land,
Has dug snow from buried paths,
Has scraped frost from an icy windscreen,
And felt the sting of arctic blasts.
Summer heat? Bring it on!
I'll take it while it lasts!

Music

Music can take you back through time.
It can heal an aching heart.
It mystically talks to all walks of life;
It gives sound to the world of art.

It can make you suddenly catch your breath
With a merging of silence and sound.
It can start a pounding in your chest
Where only silence was found.

It can bring a smile or a tear to an eye.
It can cry for all broken hearts.
It can bring peace to the fearful;
Be a tool that unites broken parts.

It can bring new ideas that are wordless.
It can conjure the sounds of the Earth.
It can put you in touch with the mystical
And span piety, sorrow and mirth.

It can restart a brain that's in standby mode;
Give therapy through salvation;
Can serve as a spiritual mentor,
Regardless of age or station.

It can hold a hidden message.
It can clear a troubled mind;
Or rescue a soul stuck in cruise control,
With power and love enshrined.

It holds magic beyond the notes that are heard;
Can ease pain and quiet the heart.
A single note can send you reeling,
Allowing new notions to start.

It can show all the colours of the rainbow
And give freedom to the forlorn.
It is awesome to peer into music's heart...
Where so many wonders are born.

The Replacement

Clarry was twenty. She was petite; fresh-faced and exuded an appealing kind of innocence.

She had found Roland's note after a particularly gruelling day at the office. It leapt out at her as she came through the front door. It was horrible. It was ugly. It was, without doubt, the most selfish and underhanded thing that had ever come into her young life.

Clarry had cried for days. She had sat sobbing each morning before leaving the flat for the bus, resumed her grief when she got home, and cried herself to sleep with awesome regularity. For two weeks she had left the evil paper sticky-tacked to the mirror, just inside the front door, where she had found it.

Occasionally she would pull it off and go over the words again. On some of these occasions she couldn't get passed *'Clarry, I'm sorry to have to tell you like this...'* She would press it back to the glass, stagger a few steps, fall face down on the little settee, where she would sob uncontrollably.

---oOo---

After a couple of weeks the hurt and anger began to subside. The evening was cold. She sat with a hot drink, staring at a blank TV screen. There was nothing she wanted to watch and was content to sit, quietly contemplating her situation. It had been another hectic day in the office and was happy to just relax and take stock. She certainly liked her work and had no intention of changing that. She thought about how this, at least, was a stable part of her life. What had the Desiderata said? 'Keep interested in your own career, however humble; it is a real possession in the changing fortunes of time.' How right that was! Her father had made her learn this off by heart as a youngster. He made it a fun thing; not a chore. He was always quoting pieces from it. She smiled at her childhood.

Across the room the CD rack caught her eye; it had gaps. She got up and stood staring at what was missing. The rack seemed to give her an evil, toothy grin; the gaps which had held Roland's compact discs stood out like missing teeth. It was strange how she hadn't noticed this before. She wandered into the bedroom. The wardrobe door swung open with a jangle of empty hangers. Standing at the bedside she looked down at the side table. She stood staring at a series of oval stains, where Roland had been clumsy with his bottle of cologne; kept there for their 'special occasions'. He was also clumsy in bed. Did she miss the intimacy? She didn't know. He wasn't a gentle person; or lover. She opened a drawer in the dresser and took out a photo album. She held it to her breast and went back to the table in the lounge and sat down.

She sipped at her cold tea, and told herself, as she had done a number of times that she needed to get a grip; so far that hadn't really helped. She also told herself she had several options. She could move back home; her parents would be happy with that, but that wouldn't do, she needed to move forward. She could get a pet. She loved cats, and since moving out from home she had really missed the company of the cat she had grown up with. Roland had probably been some sort of replacement… she shuddered. She flipped absent-mindedly through the photos. Happy family shots looked back at her. She had kept up her weekly calls home, but she didn't have to explain any of this… not yet. More pictures; some of old class-mates. At school she had taken up the cello. She remembered how well she had done; and the praise that was heaped on her by her music teacher.

Something in her stirred.

---OOO---

The next morning she got off the bus at an early stop and wandered into a quiet part of town. She found herself staring through the window of a music shop, her pulse quickening. The cello was simply exquisite; beautifully shaped with a rich, brown, glossy finish… and before the day had passed, it was hers.

---OOO---

For the next few days she was happy to let it lean in the corner of the bedroom. On the following weekend she flicked through the Yellow Pages, stuck a pin in the page for music teachers and booked her first lesson.

Mister Beauvais was French, very French. He had a small, aging figure, but was filled with fire. He was strict, with a passion for music; but his old eyes could sparkle and he had a boyish sense of humour. His fees were reasonable and he lived an easy bus ride from the flat. Within a couple of lessons she had found where she was at school, and beyond. He would say "Remember, Clarissa..." He always used her full name. He told her that her name came from the French and Latin before that. It had been Clarus, which meant clear and bright, and this is how he wanted her instrument to sound. 'Remember," he would say, "hold your elbows high like an eagle's and let your bow flow like water". He told her she showed a great deal of promise.

---oOo---

The weeks passed quickly now, with each lesson being punctuated with a series of minor victories. With her bow technique improving, she found that the simple practice pieces were slowly merging with far more sophisticated and challenging works by Bach, Haydn and Vivaldi. She regularly practiced at home, but with a greatly reduced volume. She would pull the chair out from the table, set up her music stand, sit looking into the centre of the room, and let her cello sing. Its voice was smooth, rich and deep. Mister Beauvais had emphasised that a cello needed to be played loudly to keep up with other instruments, giving the example that the flute produces the power of four cellos; but here... in her tiny flat, its soft low tones would avoid any unpleasantness with her neighbours.

Clarry continued to practice every spare minute she had. As soon as she got home in the late afternoons she would rush to her cello and play for hours, very often quite oblivious of hunger or exhaustion. She would sit, barefoot, eyes closed in rapture, hair swinging loose; she would lose herself in the bittersweet notes that floated up from her bow.

Note by note, and bar by bar, Clarry found that the ache in her heart was diminishing to the same degree that the ache in her arms and back, grew more intense. Practice was by no means easy, but she enjoyed it. Now, instead of lying awake at night reciting and analysing every word of Roland's note, she found herself engrossed in visualising the mastery of the tricky shift from G to E on her beloved instrument.

Some evenings she would even get back out of bed, take the cello from the wardrobe that had one time only contained Roland's hangers; sit on the edge of the bed and play. The tones and penetrating vibrations swirled up through her body. She could feel her every sinew buzzing with the smooth, chocolaty tones. Her tutor had told her, "You must become one with your cello; as you take it between your legs you must also take it into your heart; just as you would a man. Let the strings vibrate through your soul and let the music pour from you with passion." Several times she reflected on the fact that despite the cello's solid structure it was far softer than Roland had ever been. She would allow the rapture to engulf her as the music flowed; then slowly, she would lovingly put the instrument away and crawl into bed, exhausted.

---OOO---

Around three months had passed since the worst evening of Clarry's life. Her lessons were still going well, allowing her to accomplish more and more difficult things. The spaces in the CD rack had filled up gradually, with exotic sounding names like Paganini, Dvorak, Janacek, and Schumann.

She was playing one of these CDs when the phone rang. It was Roland. She froze. His voice was thick with slurring words. He seemed to be asking if he could come round 'to see if she was alright', followed by something not quite audible about having missed her. She thought she heard the word 'mistake' but couldn't be sure as most of it was drunken mumbling. Before Clarry had a chance to say anything, Roland's drunken state caused him to cut himself off.

Clarry wasn't really interested in whether he would call back; besides, she had nothing to say to him. She replaced the receiver, unplugged the phone at the wall, and went back to Vivaldi.

---oOo---

As she lay in bed that night she gazed at her cello through the semi-darkness of the bedroom. Of late she had taken to leaving the wardrobe door open. It was glowing in the light from the streetlamp outside the bedroom widow; the glossy lacquer glowed with a special beauty. She was still a little unsettled by Roland's call. She lit her bedside lamp, got out of bed, and tenderly removed the cello. Then, sitting on the edge of the bed with the cello imprisoned between her thighs, her thumbnail plucked a single string. A deep, delicious tone vibrated up through her body; like electricity. After a long pause, while yet again taking in this latest turn of events, she started to play.

The arc of her arm swept faster and faster as she played the opening movement of Chopin's Cello Sonata. Agile fingertips danced across the slender neck. The vibrant tones wrapped around her like a warm blanket in the cool night air. Her hair swept from side to side and her forehead glistened with beads of perspiration. Finally, with all passion spent, she returned to her bed. She laid the cello down next to her, coiled up against the smooth curve of its side, and drifted off into a sound sleep.

In the morning, Clarry woke to find her arm still lying across the cello. She smiled, kissed its belly, rolled out of bed, took Roland's note from the mirror and burnt it in the kitchen sink.

The Sight of a Tree

Who is it that has not in some quiet moment
Stood near, and paid homage to a tree?
With its roots drawing life from the riches beneath,
A wonder you never see.

Who is it that hasn't felt the majesty,
Or been awed by a leafy scene,
Or struck by their calm rectitude?
All dressed in majestic green.

How comforting is their presence,
And what assurance they seem to bring,
With flowing sap filling sky-bound veins,
Each tower, a breathing thing.

These sentinels that stand and watch in silence
Give life in so many ways,
With their whistling screams of a thousand needles
To the rustle when a sapling sways.

Such dynamic and unstoppable growth
Anchored so deep in the ground.
Their very existence is a work of art;
A miracle so easily found.

Who hasn't felt the bark of a trunk?
Known the strength so plain to see.
Felt glad that it stands the test of time,
Or just joy... at the sight of a tree.

Serenity

It is hard to pursue serenity;
Or even describe the way
One seeks an elusive opening,
With no signs in the passageway.

Does one look for some hidden oasis,
Or a sparkling ocean of dreams?
Does it hide in a vale of shadows,
Barely lit by soft moonbeams?

Is it found when the wind whispers through leaves,
Or scribed in some ageing scroll?
Can it only be found on hallowed ground,
Or the most perfect part of a soul?

Is it something only a few attempt;
That only a few can feel?
Does it engender some inner grace
That only a God can reveal?

Can it be heard in a wave of music,
Or smelt in an opening bloom?
Can it be felt through life's endless dance,
Or only where swirling dreams loom?

Does it glitter and swirl in a singing sea,
Or float down from a soaring sky?
Can it be tasted in salt-laden air,
Or do magical potions apply?

It must be a place with no challenge to face,
And where passions are not pursued.
A place where no hurry is found;
Where earthly things can't intrude.

For serenity settles in a moment quiet;
One that burdens will not allow.
A single moment that does not move on.
It has no past or future... just a now.

Knowing Where To Look

The man from World Magazine knew in his bones he had found someone who could tell him what had actually happened, out there on the island... find out what had taken place all those years ago that led to it now being a place of pilgrimage.

The old man smiled and tapped his glass. The journalist got up and went to the counter. He returned with two glasses of ice-cold spring water; a local product.

"Where was I now?" the old man mumbled, as he raised the drink slowly to his lips. "Ah! Yes, the island; where it all began."

The reporter turned his notebook to a fresh page. He had come a long way to get this story and he wasn't about to miss anything now.

"In truth, the island is only small and surrounded by a vast sea. It's picturesque enough, but has very little fertile land. Its coastline consists of rocks pulverized by the tides; with daily battering of wind and wave. As a result of its isolation, back then you could have said that it was a good place for contemplation, and meditation. An attribute not readily appreciated by many of the residents at the time. The village consisted of a couple of hundred simple souls, trying to eke out a living from a tiny cultivated strip that ran down the island's centre."

He paused, lacing his ancient fingers with deliberation.

"I should tell you about Bolo. He lived in the village on his own, but was friendly and on good terms with everyone. He was a somewhat timid and cautious young man as far as other people were concerned, but he was always ready to help anybody in need."

"Anyway, it came about, after much discussion, that the villagers decided they needed to have some spiritual guidance from a learned person; someone who could guide them through the troubled waters of their island existence. They were mostly illiterate peasants, and had no idea about what holy books contained. Their wisdom could only be based on the knowledge gathered through the experiences of their everyday lives."

"You mean there was no religion on the island?" the reporter interrupted.

"Not at that point, no." The old man went on, "It was quite amazing really; they began to build a temple with their own labours. They all contributed enthusiastically both with materials and manual labour. It turned out to be a most handsome wooden construction overlooking the village, and having a wide panoramic view of the sea, with all its changing moods and colours."

"They persuaded a Buddhist priest from the mainland to serve in their temple, to provide teachings and spiritual guidance in their times of need and emotional weakness. It pleased them that they considered they had found a good priest, who was not greedy and accepted rudimentary board and lodging at the temple in return for spiritual guidance. The villagers agreed to provide him with food, homespun clothing and at times a few coins for occasional trips back here to the mainland."

"One day a week the priest gave talks, based on the scriptures of our Lord Buddha, and he answered any questions posed by the villagers. The peasants were happy to have something more in their lives; something beyond the daily labours and their farmlands. On the days of these teachings they would finish their work early and flock to the temple. Bolo thought himself an illiterate who would have no any idea or have any comprehension about higher teachings and avoided going to the temple to listen to the sutras; but, in time he was persuaded by others to go along."

"The priest would recite from a sutra, a sermon given by Buddha to his audiences. Bolo could not understand a single word of the sutra, which was being recited in its original Sanskrit, but afterwards the priest would translate into the language of the peasants, and it all began to make sense. It analysed human life with all its daily hard living, and its suffering. As the recitation proceeded Bolo found it interesting and absorbing. He had never analysed life in such a way before. He was pleased to learn that the human spirit was not a complicated thing at all. He wished he was not illiterate and was able to read the original sermons for himself. The next best thing was to listen to it through the interpretation of the high priest, and to this end he focused his mind on each and every word. So, that's the way it went. The priest recited and Bolo listened; with great interest."

"Whenever he got home, he found the words kept reverberating in his mind and slowly he began to appreciate them as words of great wisdom, to be appreciated only by a receptive mind. He began to visit the temple more frequently and became fascinated by the man who uttered them. The priest found in him an earnest disciple in search of the truth, and began to tell him more about Buddha himself and his life. Bolo came to know Buddha as a person who was born in Northern India to a provincial king, surrounded by all the luxuries of life, as to fit a prince."

"Whenever Bolo went to the temple, he stayed behind and asked the priest to recite him more sutras uttered by Buddha and to give him a simple explanation; one that would suit a layperson like him, with a simple mind."

"You say he had a simple mind; was that really the case?" the journalist interjected.

"Oh! Yes" said the old man, taking another drink. "Anyway," he continued "more than this, the holy man would tell him stories; about Buddha the man. He loved to listen to these tales. Some of these would actually leave Bolo in a cold sweat that only left him as the breeze swept over him on his walk home."

"Although Bolo was illiterate, he began to ponder over the deeper meaning of the sutras, and soon began to acquire more sophistication in his understanding. His sincerity and devotion was very much appreciated by the priest, and as the priest talked about it to his other lay congregation, the news of Bolo's zeal and enthusiasm began to spread among the villagers at large. They would visit his home and listen to his stories as he retold them. They began to call him Sutra

Man', which Bolo did not mind at all; in fact it made him feel quite proud."

"He began to develop a real love for the Buddha and his teachings, both of which he held in high regard, and he began to consult the priest about the thorny questions about life and death. People noticed the great change that came over Bolo. He was no longer a timid person; he was becoming more self-reliant and more courageous, as if he had conquered, to some extent at least, the day-to-day fears and tribulations of his fellow man. He became amusing too, and used his humour to pass on the stories of Buddha's life to his friends and others in the village. People even began to consult him about their own personal and moral tribulations."

"As it happened, the time eventually came around for the villagers to travel to the mainland by boat to buy provisions, new seeds and general supplies. The mainland was two days away by sailing ship. The dozen or so elders on board were pleased to have Bolo along to keep them entertained with his wit and his stories of Lord Buddha."

"Yes. Yes, I see", said the journalist, holding up his hand to show that he needed to catch up. He scribbled hurriedly for a few moments, and then looked up. The old man nodded and went on.

"As they left the island the pleasant sunshine and gentle breeze created an atmosphere of calmness. After an uneventful journey, they reached the mainland and the big town. The villagers went off in different directions to gather what was needed and arranged to meet the following day on the waterfront for their return trip."

"Bolo had seen statues of Buddha in the village temple and he liked to look at them often, because they conveyed to him something beyond words. In his own, simple way, it had often occurred to him that human eyes evolved much earlier than the birth of any language, and as such, eyes may well have accumulated more knowledge than language. He also remembered the talk the priest gave about an episode from the Buddha's life."

"The story went that in the evenings, Buddha used to talk to the congregation of lay people about human life, its sufferings and of life at large in all its deeper aspects. One day he sat, and people came to pay homage and to listen to him impart words of wisdom and of human salvation. There were large numbers of people sitting there, waiting for his sermon to start. However, he did not say anything, but just sat there in meditation. Half the people got fed up and moved away. After some time he took a flower and held in his hand. Nobody understood; so they too moved away, thinking Buddha was not going to utter a single word that evening. In the end only one man was left and Buddha asked him why he was still there when others had moved away, and the man answered, 'Tonight you have given the greatest sermon of your life and it was the greatest privilege to be present.' As he said this, tears of gratitude and joy were rolling down his face. Bolo had immediately understood what the lone seeker had felt."

The old man sat with his head bent in thought. He looked up with a joyful glint in his eyes and went on.

"Well now, in the town, Bolo visited several shops that sold statues of the Buddha, but none met his expectations. Most were carved out of stone and were much too bulky, and their flat expressions did not suit his taste at all. Someone told him of a woodcarver who was a master of his craft, so Bolo went to see him."

The story teller stopped and pointed a crooked finger over the reporter's shoulder. "The shop itself is only a few doors away from where we sit."

"Anyway, truly this man was an artist and through his wonderful skills he managed to convey something of the otherworldly reality of the Buddha's looks. Bolo walked along the shelves marvelling at the shop-owner's work. He had wanted one that showed a smile, but there wasn't one; so, eventually, he settled for a magnificent piece with a high price tag. It was more than he wanted to pay, but he liked it so much that he paid the price, wrapped it in a piece of cloth and returned to the waterfront in order to board the ship. When they all met up he showed his companions his new statue. He was very proud of it. They took it in turns to hold it admiringly for a few moments before it was wrapped up to keep it from damage. Then, one by one they climbed aboard the boat."

"As the ship sailed homeward, the sky became quite cloudy, although showing no signs of danger at first. However, as the day progressed, more dark clouds built up. The villagers were looking over the sea to the distant horizon and soon saw great, black streaks across the horizon, which they took to be a portent of heavy rains and winds. Soon they saw flashes of lightening and gradually it advanced towards the ship. They were terrified of the coming storm and it soon began to rain heavily and the wind was creating huge waves. It was a frightening experience for the passengers and the captain announced that they were heading into a major storm that was then being whipped up by gale force winds."

"The people on the ship became increasingly distressed about the fate of the ship, and their own lives. They began running around the ship clutching at their meagre possessions. There was not much they could do and so huddled together in tears, moaning about their ill fate and bad karma."

"The force of the storm increased and soon they heard deep gurgling noises coming from the underside of the ship, as though the ship was breaking up. The huge waves tossed the ship like a toy; it rolled, going first one way and then the other, with great, heavy sprays of water cascading across the decks. All on board took shelter in the lower decks, clinging to the wooden benches. Some were discussing the possibility of being tossed into the open seas in the darkness, where they would surely be devoured by sharks; and how they would never see their families again."

The story teller paused to sip his drink and move around in his chair. The reporter finished jotting and looked up. "A lot of very frightened people, I imagine", he commented; then sat waiting for the other to go on.

"Yes, they were; but not all of them. In fact only the captain and Bolo seemed to keep their sanity as the storm worsened. Bolo had spread his bedding out and prepared to sleep for the night when people gathered around him asking how he could possibly sleep with the storm raging. He smiled up at them; his eyes sparkling, matching the spark that seemed to be growing deep inside him. He invited them all to sit with him, and he proceeded to tell stories late into the night."

"He told about how the Buddha's father, the king, wanted his son to become a great king, so he shielded him from any religious teachings or knowledge of human suffering. He held his audience's attention with the time Buddha had wandered out one day and was horrified to come across an old man; and how this was his introduction to old age. He told about how Buddha had slipped away from the palace, assisted by his charioteer while the hooves of the horses were muffled by the gods to prevent detection. His audience was held spellbound as Bolo described how an evil man named Devadatta had tried to kill Lord Buddha by dropping a large boulder on him; and how the rock had split in two as it fell, and how Buddha had survived."

The old man stared across the table with happy eyes. "He had listened very carefully to what the priest had told him, you see? He was an excellent pupil."

The reporter stopped scribbling. Something suddenly stirred in him. "You!" he said. It was you... you were the teacher... you were the priest!"

"Yes," the old man replied, with a great, beaming smile He waved a hand. "Not any more though; I have been long retired now, and replaced by a younger man. But yes, I was the priest."

The reporter nodded reverently and said "Please go on."

"Well finally Bolo told them that there was no use panicking or crying; that they should pray to Buddha to save the ship. He said that if they were going to die, that was his will; he told them that he trusted that Buddha would protect them. With that, he went to sleep, and they followed his example. Despite the storm they all huddled together and slept soundly."

"The tempest lasted the whole night; the captain struggled relentlessly with the vessel; despite its torn sails and a broken mast."

"When morning came Bolo woke. 'Have we arrived home', he said, 'or have we arrived in the non-suffering land of Buddha's heaven?' "When he looked around at the happy faces he knew they had arrived safely."

"When Bolo reached his home he unpacked the statue and put it on a pedestal, and burnt incense before it. He called the villagers to come and pay homage and thanks to Buddha, which they did with the utmost reverence."

The priest clapped his hands together softly.

"Ah! Now we get to the part of the story you already know. The day that it happened. On that day, sunlight poured into Bolo's little room, crowded with the survivors, and the statue looked splendid in its new surroundings. I can tell you with certainty that Bolo was pleased, but not at all surprised, to see that his newly purchased Buddha was smiling back at him. Yes, it was. It was really smiling back at him..."

"Was this really a miracle?" The reporter asked abruptly.

The old priest sat back in his chair. "Well now, I have often been asked that question. I leave that for you to decide... You know, one definition of a miracle is a perceptible interruption to the laws of nature by divine intervention."

He shook his head slowly. "Oh! There have been many versions of what happened that day. Some people say that it was a trick of the light and that the villagers had not looked at the statue properly before boarding the boat, or that it got wet during the storm and its features became distorted; while others suggest that the statue was actually altered by someone during the voyage. Some have even put forward the idea that there were two statues and not one. Where do you see the miracle? People are always looking for miracles, yet life itself is a miracle!"

He leaned forward.

"I know this; lives were saved, many people found a faith and a new path to follow; a great many visitors have come to this corner of our world and we have made many new friends."

The old man repeated his question. "Well now my friend, you've heard the story, a true account of what happened; from the horse's mouth you might say. Tell me… where do you see the miracle?"

Mirror

The mirror is stood, like no mirror should,
Covered, against a wall.
With grime and gild upon its frame,
And posing no threat at all.

But oh! The things this piece has done
When residing within a house.
The evil it wrought, the lives it struck,
And the fear that none could dowse.

Nobody knew or understood
The evil that lived inside.
It was never suspected, or brought to book,
When people mysteriously died.

Many a soul now lost to this world,
Be they old or vainglorious youth,
Merely gazed, as anyone would,
Never to know the truth.

They, who looked in, felt a tug from within,
And the pull of some awesome power.
The life from the gazer was gradually spent,
Like the sap from a dying flower.

But now this room, cobwebbed and dark
Has no souls to bait the trap.
No more hearts to break, no more years to take.
No more lives to lose their sap.

It rests there still, and stay it will,
With no more souls to snare.
Its power has gone; it can do no harm
Because... nobody knows it's there!

Sitting Quietly In the Night

Sitting quietly in the night,
With all you need at hand.
Sensing a poem that burns in your head,
Like a fire that's fully fanned.

When you're answering the call, of you know not what,
With subtlety and grace fully lacking,
You can't hurry the night, when sitting alone,
Nor hasten the brain when it's wracking.

Compulsion can be a cruel mistress,
When words don't come out right.
And you know it is slow, as thoughts ebb and flow,
Sitting quietly in the night.

And when words fall out in an ugly array,
And when metaphor and cadence aren't there;
It's all you can do, for a minute or two,
To hold off the gloom and despair.

The weight of ideas can be awesome,
With brain-power not easing your plight.
When meter and rhyme aren't worth a dime,
Sitting quietly in the night.

When ideas get split, and they just don't fit,
And the words to oblivion rush,
Then… sitting quietly in the night,
New thoughts come back in a rush.

It is neither a factory nor a halcyon place,
Sitting quietly in the night.
It's a temporal lair; it's a thinking affair,
Fulfilling some inalienable rite.

Just sitting quietly in the night,
Doing nothing remotely muscular.
Like my friend, the pondering owl,
I am vigilant, immersed… and crepuscular!

A Quiet Moment

The woman slouched across to the window and tossed out yesterday's worries, along with the contents of the chamber from under her sagging bed. She moved slowly into the tiny kitchen, where she alternated puffing on a cigarette with pieces of toast. A gin was poured into a grubby coffee cup and she looked quickly away as she caught sight of her reflection in the dusty window pane. She stared, blurry-eyed at the wall clock instead, poised permanently at three twenty-five. This never really seemed to matter, but she did remember a time when the second hand moved slowly around the dial. It had always seemed to her that it was counting away her life, second by second. It was better that it was frozen.

She poured another gin and fell into the kitchen chair; the coldness of it made her back ache. She sat sipping gin and contemplating the purple needle marks up and down her arms. She found shapes that resembled animals, as a child might in clouds or embers.

She looked up and felt guilty about the four days of grimy dishes piled in the sink. She looked down at her hand and fanned her fingers. She stared at the wrinkled skin and dirty fingernails. Her mouth twitched into a half smile momentarily as she remembered a time when her skin was smooth and her eyes were bright.

The shiny little digital clock, a gift from one of her wealthier admirers, told her she hadn't long to dream about silly things. She knew she should shower away last night's visitor, but she felt too tired; besides, the water never did run really hot. She looked down at her hand again. The mark was still visible where a ring had once been. It seemed such a long time ago... such bad memories.

As she slid the gin bottle across the table she was startled by a sudden noise. This always had that affect, but she never knew why. It was a sound she had heard many hundreds of times over the years. As noises go, it was not loud or angry, but rather in reality it was soft and furtive. After all, it was just another gentle knock on her door...

Dream World

Sliding quietly into dream; to a world where anything goes.
A flicker of images on the inner eye; a state of quiet repose.

A priest lights yet another candle, with a shaking hand,
While a comet plummets down to earth,
Somehow, deciding not to land.

Abandoned fast food cartons, stretch along a moonlit road.
The words of a favorite poem being sounded by a toad.

A book that describes how to see shades;
not just black and white.
The whistle of a human cannonball, scudding out of sight.

Campers counting stars through the slit of a tent
A mislaid letter, wedged in a drain,
It was only ever sent.

Coloured ribbons tangled in a dying tree.
A young, blind lover, serenading an empty balcony.

A well fed crow morphing into a starving wren.
A broken raft sweeps down a rapid, and then back up again.

An ivy-covered cave; a sign saying 'Angels Keep Out'.
Colourless peacocks with bandy legs, stumbling about.

Fairies playing in a summer field, measuring their strides.
A dried up stream bed, where a golf ball hides.

All these scenes come tumbling in, while we are asleep.
And as we stir to life again,
Tossed back on the rubbish heap!

An Unprompted Thought

I had a thought the other day.
What prompted it, I cannot say.
An idea set down in a book.
In thought, I took another look.

A fencing teacher played his part;
Passing on his sword-play art.
Skills born in days of old.
The lesson given, the fencer's hold.

How firm the grip, it must be right.
Not too loose, not too tight.
The student needs to understand,
A bird is wrapped within his hand.

Held too tight the bird will die.
Held too loose the bird will fly.
But how much more in the burley of life
Can this rule be used to hold off strife?

Hold a loved one in an iron fist,
And their urge to escape will be hard to resist.
Allow the bond to loosen and fray,
And see the other stray away.

Hold a job in a feverish grip,
And the reason for working can easily slip.
Be too free with the spoken word,
And after a while you will not be heard.

Hold your coins in a clenched fist,
And the value they hold can cease to exist.
Praise and compliments too easily made,
Cause the power of the words to quickly fade.

So, in that approach of holding a bird
Many an echo can be heard.
So many aspects of life it seems
Can come into balance between extremes.

The artistry of a fencing master
Can avoid the chance of many a disaster.
I had this thought the other day.
What prompted it, I cannot say.

Screening

It seemed to be tall story time again in the back room of the country club. The oldest member of the group had just finished talking about some bloke he knew way back who could touch his ear with his tongue. Nobody really believed him of course, but that didn't matter. As the guy behind the bar used to say — once this mob had knocked back a couple of beers, it didn't seem to matter what stories came out.

The old guy seemed rather pleased with the effect that his story had had, and wandered off to refill his glass.

"Touching his ear!" somebody mumbled.

"Can you do better?" asked a mate, with a friendly smile.

"As it happens; yes".

The half dozen men pulled their chairs closer to the table and stared anxiously at the man with the new story.

"Thing is", he started, "this story happens to be true. It's about screening".

"Screening? What the hell's that!" asked a younger man who seemed annoyed that he had never heard of the subject.

"Screening, no, you probably don't know about it. It can take hold... take hold" he repeated softly as his eyes glazed over.

More smiles went around his audience. "Well, go on then." one of them urged.

"OK. There was this kid, you see. Leanne was her proper name, but she was just known as Lea. This kid was really into to screens. I mean, seriously into them. She'd spend hours looking at computer screens, TV screens, a hand-held game screen, mobile phone screen, cinema screen; you name it, and the chances are she's looked at it. In fact, I figured that if you gave her a piece of paper with a rectangle drawn on it, she'd probably sit staring at it; just waiting for something to happen".

"Kid sounds as if she's got it real bad" interjected the old guy as he returned with a fresh drink. He had caught the beginning of the new story with interest. He sat down and leaned forward with the others.

"Ah! Real bad you say; it gets better!" said the story teller.

"Go on then", one of them repeated.

"Well, as it turned out I was talking to her dad one day and told him what I thought. You know, about the rectangle on a piece of paper. I didn't really think any more about it. That is, not until I ran into him again and he told me he had followed up on my idea and given his daughter a small piece of card with a rectangle neatly drawn on it."

"You're kidding us!" scoffed one of his companions.

"No. It's true. But it gets better!" He slowly took a couple of swigs at his glass, looking at his mates staring at him with rapt attention as he did. He sat contemplating his beer for a moment.

"OK. It gets better. I might not believe a word your saying but I'd like to hear the rest of it. What happened... when he gave her the card I mean?"

"Well. The kid took the card and disappeared into her room. Apparently, according to her dad, she squatted cross-legged in the middle of her bed just staring at it for over an hour".

"I don't believe any of this" a new voice piped up.

"Nor do I" said another.

The older man told them to settle down. With raised eyebrows he turned to the man telling the story. "Of course, you don't expect any of us to really swallow any of this do you?"

"Well, you can think what you like. The fact is this is a true story. Anyway", he glanced around at the little gathering, "It gets better!"

"It gets better he says", the youngest member of their group was becoming visibly irritated.

"Come on", one of them said with a touch of impatience, "the rest of us want to hear what happened".

"OK. OK. As I was saying, the kid sat staring at this card-thing for over an hour. The dad said she finally came out of her room and went looking for her mother."

He paused again to take a drink. Legs shuffled beneath the table.

"He told me" he went on, "...and I can only tell you what he told me...he told me that he heard his daughter ask her mother, "Mum, this needs new batteries!"

The Upside of Pain

It's been medically and logically proven,
There is an upside to pain.
But it's hard to observe the use that it serves
When your body is giving you cane.

When asked "How much does it hurt, dear?"
It's very hard to explain.
You are asked to assess it from zero to ten
With some addled part of your brain.

If it wasn't there, to keep you aware
Of the hurt and the mental strain,
You would slowly decline, becoming supine,
With recovery hard to gain.

But the benefits of agony are hard to see
When it stabs again and again.
When your body is racked, it remains a fact
That your thoughts at least, are profane.

So when torture strikes with burns and spikes,
With composure hard to maintain,
With tongue in cheek, so to speak,
You know you're not... on a gravy train.

But whichever way you look at it,
No matter how arcane.
If by Him from above, as an act of love,
T'was a clever thing to ordain.

The Lazy Beat of Autumn

There's a lazy beat to Autumn;
A season of temperate things.
Like the gentle drone of insects unseen;
The unheard beating of butterfly wings.

Trees rustle their melodies over the warming earth,
Whispering Nature's story of old.
While dry leaves leave stark bare boughs
Dappled with orange, brown and gold.

From the contagious happiness of bird song
To the screeching flocks as they pass.
The soft, calming scent of each blossom.
The soft green smells of warm grass.

With the pastel hues of Nature's art
And the beauty of sparse clouded skies.
All creatures share a happiness
In all that the season implies.

A time of rest and renewal,
With changes running rife.
This is my favourite quarter
Of the changing chess board of life.

All the Time in the World

Gerald was a boy that had always had all the time in the world. He didn't know why his perception of time was so different to everybody else's, but he knew it was. This wasn't a problem to him; but it was to others.

"Come on slow coach" "Buck up there, kid!" "Move yourself Gerald, you're holding everybody up!" All typical chides and complaints that had taunted his life for as far back as his memory could go; for as long as Gerald had marched to the beat of a different drum.

These reprimands were from grownups of course, other teenagers seem to see it differently. Not a weakness so much as an amusement; a thing to taunt, something to joke about. After all, kids didn't get all wound up about it the way adults tended to.

Gerald knew that if you take more time, you are able to observe, rather than just see, the things and events that surround you. As a general rule Gerald kept his notions about time to himself, but knowing that his feelings about it seemed to be so different to other peoples he had made a project of it; reading about, and thinking about, what time actually was.

For instance, he knew form his class lessons that the planet, its rivers, seas, mountains and valleys had all been formed and shaped over millions of years. He knew that there was something called tectonic movement way beneath his feet that gradually shunted particles around with incredible slowness to ultimately bring about vast ruptures in the planet's landscape.

He had seen this show, on telly, about a tribe in South Africa. The commentator was explaining how this old Zulu guy had sent word to his friend in a village far away that he wanted to meet him and discuss tribal matters.

So, his friend starts walking. He walks for two or three days, Gerald couldn't remember exactly, but a long time. He finally gets to the place where they are supposed to meet. The re-enactment of this shows the man arriving at the spot, laying an old blanket down under a tree to wait. Gerald had watched the show with tears in his eyes as the tribesman settled down with a pipe, watching the desert sky grow dark, knowing that his friend would arrive later in the night, or the following day, or the day after that!

The next morning his family seemed to be running more than usually late. His mother was panicking; his father drove off without waiting for the food she had prepared. Gerald, being the only child, had tried to help his mother, but his slowness had only made things worse.

As he walked the short distance to school that morning his head swam dizzily with the rush of the society he found himself living in. He imagined a million alarm clocks buzzing and chiming in a million homes; the rush to the bathroom, the dressing, eating, hurrying to the bus or train or car or...

Gerald's head swam with these visions as he tried to relate these different worlds; these different perceptions of time.

On the one hand it was about the flow of seasons and the never-ending, yet unhurried cycle of sunlit days; together with the predictable and comforting waxing and waning of a village moon.

On the other, it was all about the alarm clocks.

These events had been some sort of turning point for him; and so his study of all things time-related had taken on a whole new meaning.

Despite his youth, Gerald had realised that these two perceptions of time in some way encompassed the entire history of the human race, from the earliest moments of awareness as cave-dwellers and hunters-gatherers in prehistoric forests right up to the frantic, high tech, digital world he was now a part of. He could see how each human's life is deeply affected by time and its measurement, without really knowing or understanding what time actually is.

It would be true to say that these ideas, together with his obsession for gaining a greater understanding of what it was that made him different, also resulted in him becoming a loner. He had no problem with that; none at all.

In that year, his final year at school, he had paid great attention to a book he had found in the library about the creation of the universe, suggesting that time did not exist before the Big Bang, and how in some distant future the universe would stop expanding and collapses back in on itself.

He read works by the Greek philosopher Aristotle, where he defined time in terms of the change that mortals are constantly coping with, and how change is dependent on time and that without time, there would be no change.

His science teacher had given a talk about Isaac Newton, who he had described as the Father of Modern Science. He explained that Newton had seen time as that dimension of the universe in which events occur in sequence. He believed it to be an absolute; a thing unchangeable and immutable.

On the other hand his readings on the ideas put forward by Albert Einstein showed that he saw time as relative, not absolute, that it changes when affected by other forces in the universe like gravity and motion. His Theory of Relativity demonstrated that the faster you go, the slower time passes!

Although these studies had been gratifying; however, none of it could prepare him for what was about to happen. But there again, it didn't need to.

The whole thing occurred just a few weeks before break up, in the last year of his school life. A simple thing, really... a fire had started in the school. It began in a cupboard where cleaning materials were kept, eventually exploding and engulfing the two main corridors with incredible speed. For some reason the automatic sprinkler system had not activated and the fire tore through the building so fast that pupils were trapped in sections with no means of escape.

Gerald had been in the library when those who were able to, came running and screaming past the door. He heard a boy shout that the sprinklers were not working, so he made his way to the large panel across the hall and opened it.

Tools were sitting beneath the mass of pumps, meters and wires and he saw that some maintenance work was in progress. Having no idea what he was looking at, Gerald slowly picked up the fuses that sat in the tool box and pushed them one by one into empty sockets. After a few moments cold water struck the back of his head. Through artificial rain, Gerald returned to the library, picked up his pile of books and left through the front door, just as the three fire engines pulled up.

Gerald's world changed. It was not a case of him disliking the media attention, or the change in the attitude towards him by classmates, or from grown ups he had never met, or indeed his own parents.

It was more about none of them understanding his very personal issues with time. He, as an old Zulu villager, but somehow living with a million alarm clocks, found the chasm that separated him from his fellow beings had become wider.

He knew that eventually this new complication in his life would all blow over. It would take time… but of course… Gerald had all the time in the world.

Dappled With Shadow and Light

Ideas topple or balance in the brain,
With synapses dark and bright.
Like the flickering of a canvas screen,
Dappled with shadow and light.

Ideas come from darkened caves.
They burst out sharp and bright;
Crackling wires within the skull
Provide notions both wrong and right.

The source of human wisdom
Spills out from an empty space.
Either waves of evil, or flashes of good,
Passing quickly through time and space.

Jumping ideas are like water and flame;
Brains cells like fire and ice.
Light stands still, while shadows creep over
This pulsing storage device.

Notions are both whole and inseparable,
Flickering like day and night.
People have light and shadow both,
Their flashes both black and white.

The shadows range from grey to grey,
While light spans from candle to sun.
Light gives shape to images,
Shadow provides depth to each one.

The racing of day and the creeping of night
Mirror the charges that buzz through the wires.
A magical weaving of the fibres of now;
With an idea's birth that inspires.

Take all of this into reasonable account,
Applying what paradigm you might.
And you're left with the sum of human knowledge,
All dappled with shadow and light.

The Silent Observer

He's majestic and wise there's no doubt of that,
With little to cause him concern.
He sleeps all day and hunts through the night,
With a copious supply of midnight
oil; oil he is happy to burn.

He sits aloft while creatures scurry;
Not knowing they could be a feed.
Then he drops and swoops in a silent glide.
With a precision guaranteed.

This king of the night is related to hawks.
An old being, with an all-knowing look.
His kind is found all over the world.
A master, by hook or by crook.

He mostly sits without a sound,
In his dark, soft feathery gown.
He uses his acute perception of depth,
Then softly and silently sails down.

He's a masterful hunter, but few hunt him.
His eyes only look to the front.
From side to side, his whole head moves,
Like a radar that sweeps for the hunt.

Whether forest or tundra, the owl sits still,
Taking in his crepuscular view.
He sees and hears, but doesn't say much.
Just an eerie too-wit-too-woo.

What lies behind this silent observer?
What magic is held unseen?
With the reflection of moonlight in his mystic eyes;
In an age-old, enchanted scene.

This statuesque bird, by sages revered,
Holds an ancient magic within.
He knows all there is to know of the stars...
And the night belongs to him.

Beyond the Lever

He gently pressed the little wooden leaver. A soft clicking filled the room as the two men watched the metal ball run and tumble down a series of wooden channels.

After a few moments it came silently to rest in a tiny cradle at the base of the ball-run.

"That's really great!" said the visitor.

"Yes. I like it'" said the man who had laboured for many hours building the contrivance they were both staring at.

"Oh, I'm sure you do," remarked the visitor. "After all, you built it."

"Well, that's not always the case."

"What do you mean?"

"It's just that people don't always like what they build or create, do they?"

The visitor thought for a moment. "No, I suppose not. But if that's the case, why do you like this?"

"I'm not sure you really want to know the answer to that question," said the other as he blew imaginary dust from several of the channels.

"Try me."

"Well, this contraption revitalises my personal belief in the existence of the Almighty."

The other smiled. "I'm sure you have some illusive rationale for making a statement like that."

"OK, put it this way; although there is a huge disparity in the scale and complexity of...", he paused.

"Yes, scale and complexity...?"

"Well, although mere mortals such as we might find it difficult to compare such things, when you think of it, this device functions quite adequately but really serves no real purpose."

"Oh, I see; and you're comparing that with the creation of the universe?"

"Uh, yes. Something like that."

Just then, a tune played in the visitor's pocket.

"Oh! Excuse me." The man turned away and mumbled a few acknowledgements into his mobile phone. He turned back.

"Got to go, sorry. Have to pick her up now."

As he passed through the front door the visitor turned to his friend and said, "You always were weird!"

"Thanks" said the man, closing the door and hurrying back to his room.

As he entered he was filled with the burning desire to once again gently press the little wooden lever.

Stillness

In this, our present and physical world,
Is there a valid state of still?
Some past or future stillness
Could possibly fit the bill.

To quietly lay down the mind;
To let stillness abound.
Yet stillness has no vibration or rhythm,
Stillness makes no sound.

Goals and aims and strivings
Have no place in stillness at all.
No whisper abides in stillness,
No sound; no matter how small.

Small movements can be felt,
That follow a clock's last tick.
Or the imperceptible swelling of a buried seed;
But what the measuring-stick?

All attributes of stillness
Lay hidden in a buzzing world.
A beam of light is yet not still,
No mysteries here unfurled.

Stillness knows no urgency,
For stillness has no shape,
It possesses no colour, time or place,
No capture or escape.

It seems that movement is ever a part
Of the natural order of things.
With no movement at all in stillness,
Just a mystic potential it brings.

When the bolt is fully shot
And the shackle is held fast.
With the world no longer turning;
Into a void all is cast.

It is hard to fully imagine
That a held breath is truly still.
Or that the here and now ceases to move,
Driven only by will.

There is always a strange and powerful nature
In something not quite understood.
But the value of searching to comprehend,
Is presumed to be all to the good.

When Words Don't Rhyme

A thing that drives me to despair,
When finding a lack of sounding care,
My nerves are jangled every time
I read a poem where words don't rhyme.

Why are such thoughts made so plain?
Why no music in each refrain?
At once the beauty turns to grime,
When a poet's words just don't rhyme.

Is it sloth that the writers use?
Does it bode some smug abuse?
To fall so flat after such a climb.
When a stanza's words refuse to rhyme.

Can the cause be seen as haste?
Does it mean no time to waste?
You may as well express with mime.
When a group of words cannot rhyme.

Why the lack of simple care?
Why pen lines that seem so bare?
Such lowborn lines are past their prime,
When the words of a verse cease to rhyme.

To turn such lovely words to chat,
I wonder where the writer's at.
Like a weed that once was thyme,
When the chosen words don't rhyme.

It always seems to be demeaning,
Such ragged clothes for special meaning.
The message no longer sounds sublime
When selected words just don't rhyme.

Be it short or be it long,
The words need to form a song.
It comes across as such a crime,
When a poem's words don't rhyme.

Layered Perceptions

The squat house stood alone near the cliff's edge. It had been built on the rippling rock surface that ran along the landmass, high above the sea. For this reason it looked very solid, giving the impression of permanency. It was only used as a holiday retreat, so it stood empty. It was a large, square box-like building with a flat roof, almost devoid of features, with the original white painted exterior, now showing a few dark, weathered patches, slowly yellowing with age.

The entity hovered for a while; then slowly swung around it, viewing it from all angles. The entity was curious. Having drifted in from a never-ending seascape, this was something the alien could take in with an increased sense of wonder.

The capsule had come down and entered the ocean without warning, but this was in no way an immediate problem for three very good reasons. The distress signal would have been sent automatically the moment the craft made contact with planet Earth, summoning a replacement, something normally avoided at all costs; secondly, any evidence of the craft's existence would be erased within moments of the impact, and last, but most importantly; the entity had no physical form or presence of any kind. In other words, nobody knew it was there.

It moved slowly to the door and studied the rough wooden panels set in the face of it. It drifted forward, momentarily becoming one with it; then soundlessly, and without disturbing any molecules, passed through into a short hallway. As it drifted, it analyzed the peeling wallpaper, the two fading prints of people enjoying seaside holidays, and an assortment of children's renderings, tacked up in a seemingly random fashion along the hall.

If such an emotion could be attributed to this alien being, it would have to be excitement. The opportunity to study such things this closely was very rare. It knew that the response to the distress call would come rapidly, and it's time in this place would be short. For this reason alone, it moved on.

The room at the end was bathed in a more natural light, not that this had any relevance for this particular observer. The room held many wonders for the visitor. Without knowing, or for that matter, without needing to know what it was looking at, it swept past a sink with taps, open surfaces, towels, clothes, a sponge, several hanging utensils, and a row of cupboards set half way up the wall. The cupboard doors were familiar, in that they seemed to be smaller versions of the door that was embedded in the front wall of the building.

The cupboard chosen was only one of several; but this one was extra wide with grubby marks around the handle, indicating that it was probably the most used. It passed through, scanning the interior, finding lots of smaller items. Almost everything found there was made of different materials. If excitement was the relevant word for it, this was growing. Somehow, the smaller the articles, the greater was the sense of wonder and interest for the being trying to make sense of them. The molecular studies that had occupied this ethereal being early in its life cycle could well account for the inquisitive approach it now made.

The shelf that held the greatest amount of bric-a-brac, despite it being made of a thick plank of wood, bowed visibly under the weight. A great deal of the kitchen's bits and pieces had been haphazardly loaded onto the shelf with no apparent sequence or order. This aspect of the find seemed to heighten the alien's curiosity. Aside from all the pots, jugs, bowls and general china, a long plastic tray sat centrally, adding even more to the bow of the timber.

The tray was piled high with small items, seemingly thrown in at the last minute with no thought of any value attached to them, or any concern about such things being damaged. It was, in short, a tray of junk. These were just unwanted items that by some strange twist of fate had escaped the rubbish bin. One by one, each item was meticulously examined and scrutinized. A brightly coloured, plastic box seemed to contain yet another assortment of oddly-shaped articles. All this was taking time of course, and it knew that time must be running short.

The box had a hinged lid and contained what seemed to be some sort of collection. The kind of objects a young child would collect; things found in the grass or on the beach. There were buttons, small pebbles, a few bottle caps, and several pencil stubs. Tucked into one corner of the tray was a small paper bag. To our intruding being this all represented a wonderful opportunity to study such small and normally, quite unnoticed items; this being carried out in such close proximity that under any other circumstances would simply not be possible.

The bag contained shells; seashells of all colours, textures, shapes and sizes; although the sizes were generally tiny. Each shell was different; some round, some oblong, some curved, some flat. The surfaces also varied greatly; some smooth, some rough, some with heavy striations, others with a delicate ripple across the surface. In fact, it was such a shell that immediately came under intense scrutiny.

The shell was very small, almost flat, and dark grey with an almost imperceptible ripple across its surface. The alien seemed to be considering it with a near-molecular approach. In examining the ridges across the surface, a small, single grain of salt came into view. A single grain of what the being understood to be a cubic crystal of sodium chloride. This creature was now dreading the inevitable shrill sound and high-frequency vibration that would announce the sudden and instant relocation to a replacement capsule, putting an end to what could only be described as an adventure... in anybody's terms.

The salt particle rested on the darkly striped surface. It was close to being a perfect example of a crystalline solid, a structure with a three-dimensional collection of individual atoms. It was a simple, dice-like, six-sided, almost translucent cube. It was light yellow with minute blotches; these being the cause of the imperfection. The scientist in the alien was taking over from his role as terrestrial observer as the crystal was seen in some unearthly state of totality. It had several dark markings, the most intriguing being the rectangular shape centered at the base of one side. The shape, and the patterns within it, was not at all dissimilar to the rough wooden panels seen at the front of the house earlier.

A full sense of realisation of the significance of this discovery struck the strange visitor like a thunderbolt just as the inevitable shrill sound and high-frequency vibration caused a momentary tremor... and in a moment... in one brief, silent moment... it was gone.

It's An Image

Is it really just social and cultural forces
That dictate how a body presents?
With a magazine's gloss, along with stardom's dross,
Expectations become intense.

Probably not so much for him.
It seems harder to reveal
His desire to set the world on fire,
With abs like rippling steel.

But for her... the desirable body.
The dream of a perfect form.
Those sensuous curves with a blemish-free skin;
Something way beyond any norm.

Such ethereal dreams of perfection.
Such a striving for the ideal.
A body shaped like an hourglass;
Thus creating sensual appeal.

Creams and potions, cosmetics and lotions;
Products to use every day.
A need to keep trim, machines at the gym.
A body ideal; come what may.

With aerobics and Zumba, workouts and Tai chi.
With runs on a treadmill each morning.
With weights and carbs, calories and pills.
Does anyone hear the soft warning?

Mirror, mirror on the wall,
Don't you see heart, soul, and mind?
All this straining and grunting, with model-look hunting,
Can't it all be left behind?

While maintaining a smile, with some elegant style,
Through the heartache and the scrimmage;
When the neglected soul within has long gone,
All you have left... is an image!

Twinkle, Twinkle, Super Star

Twinkle, twinkle, super star,
How I wonder what you are.
Up upon the screen so high,
Like an idol in the sky.
Twinkle, twinkle, super star,
How I wonder what you are!

When the flickering image is gone,
When there's nothing to heap praise upon.
Then your life becomes most trite.
Common life must really bite.
Twinkle, twinkle, super star,
How I wonder what you are!

Then the admirer in the street
Smiles his praise as eyes meet.
This thrill could not be thus unfurled,
If you did not fill his world.
Twinkle, twinkle, super star,
How I wonder what you are!

You slip into obscurity,
No more to a hero be.
With the glitz and glamour spent,
Comes a mundane life and sad descent.
Twinkle, twinkle, super star,
How I wonder what you are!

Ifs

Trevor was something of a guru. IT was his life; with very little else holding much interest for him. In his mid thirties he was now heading up his small, yet highly successful Internet Support Company. He now sat in his office a little after business hours, waiting for his visitor.

The man due to call in was not a regular client. In fact, Stan was the sort of person that Trevor would normally have nothing to do with. But this was not normal. Nothing about what was going to take place was normal.

Stan wouldn't be happy. Not happy about being summoned by a complete stranger, even if he was intrigued. Maybe there was something in it for him. Curiosity alone would see him keep the appointment.

There was a tap at the door.

"Come in." Trevor called out.

The large, brutish figure of Stan lumbered into the room looking bewildered.

"Please take a seat Stanley."

"Stan."

"Pardon?"

"Stan, just Stan."

"Sure Stan, whatever you say." Trevor smiled and nestled back into his chair, eyeing the man with obvious caution.

He started. "I'd like to talk to you about ifs. Can I tell you about ifs?"

Stan glared.

"Funny things ifs", he went on. "Have you ever heard of the 'if statement'?" he didn't wait for a reply. "No - probably not. An If Statement is used in computer programming to make certain things happen, but only if something is true. Anyway, these ifs do actually concern you quite personally."

Stan was annoyed by the fact that none of this was making any sense. He said "What the heck are you talking about?"

"Well, that's the point of you being here isn't it? If I tell you about ifs, you'll know what I'm talking about."

Stan grunted. "Go on."

"It all started a couple of days ago. If my car hadn't refused to start, I wouldn't have been at home looking up bus times". He pursed his lips, thinking. "If I hadn't been sitting by the window reading the local bus timetable, one that I keep for such emergencies, I wouldn't have seen the dog in my back garden."

"What the hell are you talking about?" Stan interjected.

Trevor ignored the question. "If I hadn't gone out to chase it off, I wouldn't have tripped and put a very nasty gash in my leg; and if the wound hadn't swollen up so quickly I wouldn't have had a taxi take me off to the local hospital's emergency department, to get it looked at... and to have tetanus shot."

Stan started to get up saying "What kind of a nut are you? You're crazy; I don't have to listen to this!"

"Well, it's your choice of course, but like I said on the phone, what I have to tell you does affect you directly".

Stan scowled again and sat down.

"Get on with it."

"As I was saying, there I was, sitting in the waiting room. If I hadn't been sitting there I would not have had the time to read an account of last weekend's jewelry robbery, and about how a man serving in the shop had died from injuries he received during the robbery, and how the case had moved on from robbery to murder."

"Who the hell are you?" Stan shouted.

Trevor held up a hand and continued.

"If I had not been there, I certainly wouldn't have met an old school friend on my way out."

"If this meeting hadn't taken place I wouldn't have been invited to join him and another old school friend for a drink the following day. I hope you are getting the picture Stan."

Stan sat rigidly, saying nothing.

Trevor continued with his story. "At that little get together, if I hadn't got lost going to the bathroom, I would never have found myself in a poorly lit hallway, outside a room listening to a conversation. Where I heard you discussing with someone where you had put the proceeds from a robbery."

The other man started to rise again.

"Please be patient, you really do need to hear the rest of this."

Again, Stan resumed his seat.

"If I hadn't been standing there at that time I would not know how you arranged for the other man to collect the money tomorrow and meet up again after."

"If I hadn't waited down the hall, and seen the flower pinned to your collar, my old school friend wouldn't have been able to tell me who you were."

"If he hadn't identified you, I wouldn't have been able to look up your number. ...and if had hadn't been able to do that; well I couldn't have asked you to meet me here at my office, could I?"

Stan, now red in the face and seething with anger spluttered, "Who the hell do you think you are; and who's going to believe any of this?"

"Well, a good question. If I hadn't given details of this to the detective in charge of the case; and if a couple of uniformed officers hadn't recovered the money this afternoon, not many people would have believed me, I suppose."

The man stood, knocking over the chair and pulled a knife from his pocket. "And what if I make sure you don't get to any satisfaction from all your interference? I've killed once — one more shouldn't make any difference."

"Well, there is another if. If I hadn't arranged for the detective to be in the next room before you arrived I may well have come to some harm."

The door to the next room opened slowly, revealing the detective pointing a hand gun at the criminal's head.

"Drop the knife!" He barked.

The weapon clattered to the floor, and two uniformed policemen came in with handcuffs.

After the man had been lead away, the detective made his way to the door. He paused on the way out, turned to Trevor and said, "Thanks again for all your help. Would you mind coming in to the station tomorrow to give a full statement?"

Trevor grinned, and said "Yes; if you like".

The Here and Now

Where and when is the here and now.
Do we need to stop and think?
To analyse this transfixed state
Can take you to the brink.

Sand is paused in the hourglass
While the compass slowly spins,
And time and place are frozen;
Now, nothing new begins.

Nothing moves or changes course,
Nothing relocates,
There are no memories of things before,
No thought of future states.

It is merely just a moment.
It has no start or end.
Not an easy thing to see;
Hard to comprehend.

There is no anchor to hold it there;
No dilution through time and space.
No echo or vibration;
Nothing to embrace.

There can be no evolving pattern;
No progressive devouring of time.
No sense of durability.
Nothing lowly or sublime.

It's an empty piece of time
In a vanished point in space.
No sense of prolongation.
No semblance of place.

Where and when is the here and now;
With nothing to persist.
Do we need to stop and think?
Can such a state exist?

Rhythms

There are rhythms that are plain to see;
Seen by one and all.
There are some that have no look or feel,
Whether large or small.

There's the obvious ticking of a clock
And the ringing of a bell;
The clicking of computer keys;
A fairground spruiker's yell.

High heels clicking on a parkay floor.
The turning of a page.
The throbbing of a heartbeat,
Louder, when fuelled with rage.

A hovering bird's beating wings;
The rhythm of speech.
Boots echoing in a tunnel;
Waves pounding on a beach.

The rhythm of pen on paper;
Music bouncing down a hall.
A flashing indicator light;
A birds repeated call.

The measured whispering of breath;
The sway of a rocking chair;
The tempo that rattles through a train;
The chant of an offered prayer.

A cicada in the garden;
The sobbing of a child;
The dripping down a drainpipe;
Tall grass whipping wild.

The cadence of a poem;
The spurting of a Catharine wheel;
The sway of a couple dancing;
These all have look and feel.

But there is a hidden metronome,
That works a mystic beat.
Like the silent pulse of day and night.
Where some things never meet.

The endless cycle of life and death;
Galaxies swinging round some centre.
The pulsating of a dividing cell
Where eyes can hardly enter.

The body's veiled circadian rhythms.
The tempo of the seasons.
Things that tend to lay beneath,
No matter what the reasons.

The presence of recurring doubt;
Neurons firing in the brain.
Things that tick soundless in the dark
That form an unseen chain.

Are these less obvious patterns
Meant to be harder to see?
Is there some sense in keeping them quiet?
Some cosmic conspiracy?

Do people look hard for such rhythms?
Are scientists constantly seeking?
Is there some point in searching them out?
Metaphorically speaking.

Looking for measure, pace and pulse,
Is just a hobby of mine.
To see stages and steps, with tempo and time
Is just looking for reason and rhyme.

Whatever the outcome of such musing.
Whatever ends up on the list.
With options so wide, it can't be denied,
That so many rhythms exist.

Twinky

Sherry noticed that the nocturnal conversations she was having were becoming more regular. She found them a little disturbing. After all, it wasn't rational to spend every evening talking to Twinky. Once in a while yes, but of late it had become every night. She knew that Twinky (and she had never really got used to that name) well... she knew he wasn't real.

But she had to admit he had always protected her; always been there for her. More than once he had come up with solutions to problems she couldn't have solved on her own. He did make her do things, ugly things, things she didn't want to think about. But - he was always there for her. Twinky said he would always be there for her, no matter what. How many people could she say that about? Certainly not Simon; no, when she and Simon broke up, Twinky had been there for her.

She hadn't meant to hurt her boyfriend back or anything; she wasn't a vindictive person. That's where Twinky came in. He gave her what? ...resolve, yes that's what it was, resolve. Of course, people had called around asking if she'd seen him recently. She had so 'no'. 'Not really a lie, she hadn't!

As for the man mowing the next door's lawn, starting up his machine at the crack of dawn, well, anyone would have found that so unreasonable. Then, when she had gone out in her dressing gown especially to talk to him about it, he had been so rude! Twinky fixed that little problem too. He had told her exactly what to do.

Then there was the manager at the news agents where she worked; where she used to work. Telling her she wasn't giving the customers her full attention. She said she should find work where she didn't have to deal with people all day long. The woman didn't take into account the fact that most of these people she had to put up with were complete strangers! Sherry had liked it in the shop, reading magazines - that was nice... so many magazines and all free of course. When Sherry had pointed out that too much was being expected of her and that she felt she was being underpaid, the woman turned very nasty and used some very bad language.

Well, Twinky soon sorted that sordid affair out. It was a case of déjà vu, when the police questioned her about the fact that the manager's husband had reported her missing, and it seemed that Sherry was one of the last persons to see her on the day she disappeared. There could be no doubt that the fact that she was in some way connected to all three missing persons had made the police suspicious.

Anyway, looking back, it was plain now that she had made things go horribly wrong in the case of the boy from up the street. He was for ever trampling on her pretty, little flowerbed in the front garden; and the day she caught him riding his bike through it, well, she had just snapped. Without waiting to discuss the problem with you-know-who, she took things into her own hands; hands that happened to be holding hedge-clippers at the time. She realises now that she was rash and should have consulted Twinky. It was always so much neater when he planned it out; with everything nice and tidy afterwards.

As it was, Sherry was still holding the shears when the lady across the road started screaming. Things were terribly bloody, with stuff oozing out between the kid's shoulders. His head had rolled some distance down the road and she wanted to put it back, but people (there was a fair crowd gathering now) people said that it shouldn't be touched; that they should wait for the police. The worst of it was seeing Twinky up at her bedroom window shaking his head and looking very disappointed. Would he still talk to her? Would he still be there for her?

Eventually, most of the screaming died down and the police arrived. They took her into the house for questioning. It didn't take long at all. Before she knew it she was in some sort of calico waist coat being led to the car. Sherry kept looking over her shoulder at the house, as the arresting officers pushed her into the back seat.

But she needed have worried — Twinky was already there, waiting for her.

Leaning Back Against a Wall

Leaning back against a wall,
Taking in an open sky,
I ponder on the countless wars that rage,
And wonder why.

How did we make it go so wrong,
We of the planet Earth?
With conflict rattling down the ages,
What logic gave it birth?

Is it only poets and dreamers
That see another world?
With peaceful coexistence.
With conflict all untwirled.

Can a self-destructive species
Really turn the tide?
Creating a longed for Utopia,
Setting all disputes aside.

And could there really come a time,
When like me, without real care,
A person can lean against a wall
And look up into an open sky
And only see what's there?

Imagery

There are many different types of poem,
One is known as imagery.
Each one has its place of course,
But this one's for the visionary.

There's nothing wrong with a ballad,
Free verse or an epic.
A rondeau can really please the ear;
Like the sonnet, ode and limerick.

There's a wind howling like an old man's breathing.
A meteor tumbling silently, like a darkened mirror ball.
A dappled sky, like paint splashed from an artist's brush,
Or rotting leaves sleeping, and not dead at all.

Snow falling without sound, rendering the listener deaf.
A city's lights sparkling like a web of dappled dew.
Tumbleweed pretending they know where they're going.
A dirty river gurgling like rich, brown stew.

Raindrops rattling on a tin roof, like
the soft plucking of a harp.
An owl sadly moaning for a lack of prey;
Staring eyes frozen, like a marble statue.
The subtle lyrics of insects at play.

A storm brews, while a towering cypress trembles with fear.
Soft drink bubbles are like balloons rising free.
An unmoving owl, as if painted on a porcelain cup.
A rain shower wrapping around a tree.

The mighty oak's trunk, standing like chiselled granite.
A crystal web spun across a broken window.
Grass, dead and flat like an ageing carpet.
A rainbow trying to outdo the garden flowers below.

There's early children's laughter waking
flowers from there sleep.
A willow's low branch trying to sweep leaves into a heap.
There is the black of night, not there
and everywhere at the same time.
Such are the thoughts that tumble freely through the head;
With an effort to make them rhyme.

The Glitch

The being drifted into the chamber.

"I understand you have a problem."

"Yes."

"I have rather a lot on at the moment, is it a big problem?"

"Not at the moment."

"Not at the moment?"

"Yes. At the moment it's a minor glitch."

"What have we got?"

A large panoramic screen lit up and hovered in the air.

"What life form are we looking at?"

"Human."

"Where is this?"

"Erm, a planet called Earth."

"Earth… and where is this planet called Earth?"

"A moment… there… it resides in what they have named the Solar System, in what they refer to as the Milky Way."

"Milky?"

"Yes, the Milky Way."

"Is it an important planet?"

"No. Not really."

"Is it advanced?"

"Not really."

"Then, what is the problem?"

"Right now, *he* is the problem."

Both beings studied the projected image.

"What is he doing?"

"Well, basically he is fiddling with a personal computer, using the Internet."

The other took a few moments to generate definitions for the terms being used.

"A computer using an Internet on planet Earth."

"Yes."

"So, what is he doing with it?"

"Well, he's stumbled on the program for the Galactic Wave Converter."

"Are you sure?"

"Yes. He created a loop by resetting..."

A tapping sound interrupted the explanation.

"What was that?"

"A knocking on the door to the room you are looking at."

"Has that happened before?"

"Yes, several times."

"How often does this knock occur?"

"About every two of their minutes."

"What do you make of it all?"

"Well, it has been difficult to analyse what is going on; mainly because of the vast differences between time streams, together with the poor thought process interpretations that are currently available."

"But you have an idea of what his motivations are with regards to the converter?"

"Not exactly, no."

Can you extrapolate?"

"Well, yes; to a degree."

"Tell me what you think."

"It seems that we are looking at a room in a Motel in a city called Ipswich."

"Ipswich."

"Yes, it is a city in one of Earth's smaller countries. He has set up his lap top computer to call up the program to extend a period of time; approximately thirty of their minutes. He has done this to create a loop."

"A loop... can he do that?"

"It seems he has done it. He is in the loop as we watch."

"Has anything like this ever happened before?"

"No. Not to my knowledge. Very few advanced life entities have any kind of access to it. It is very carefully controlled."

"So, how did this Earth man on a lap top in Ipswich get it?"

"Of course, I can't answer that with any certainty, but he is what is known there as a *hacker*. He writes programs, and tries to break into or corrupt other programs. Such humans as this one spend time trying to gain unauthorised access to other computer users' systems."

"Strange."

"Yes, strange; and this person has broken into the program, rewritten some of its lines of code, and set up a loop for the coming thirty minutes with the..."

The knock repeated.

"... yes, for the coming thirty minutes with the intention of capturing it, as a loop, to be rerun after the loop has played out. That way he could return and move through the same time stream whenever he wanted."

"Why would he go to all this trouble?"

"Well, as far as I am able to determine, this is during his lunch time break from a nearby company, where he works, with computers; setting them up for customers."

"I see."

"Yes. Well, he regularly, once every one of their months as far as I can tell, meets there with a woman who also works in this city. They spend time together and then they return to their respective places of work."

They both studied the screen; the man at his lap top, waiting. He seemed agitated, and was continually jabbing at keys and staring at his watch.

"Fine; nothing we can do here. I appreciate your bringing this to my attention; an interesting case. Write up your report and I'll see that it's disseminated."

The being started to drift away.

"There is more to consider here."

"There is?"

"Yes. You see, the loop…"

The knock again.

"…the loop he has created is, well, it's perpetual."

"Perpetual?"

"Yes, it will not stop. The man has no control over it. At first I wondered how long it would last, but I realised that what he has started just won't stop. He has created a loop that is truly perpetual."

"That is unfortunate for him, I can see that. Do you suggest that we take control and terminate the loop? If that is part of your report it will need to be considered very carefully. Such actions are very rare as you know. There is always a great reluctance to interfere; especially with an order as low as this one."

"This is true of course, and I would certainly recommend that action if it were possible."

"Explain *if it were possible.*"

"The control for what he has created is inside the loop. Nothing from outside the program can have any effect. Only the man himself could do that, and from what I can see he is not capable of doing that."

"Most unfortunate; but recommend it anyway. Give your report top priority."

More drifting away.

"There's more. I mean there could be more."

"Yes."

"As I said, this is a minor glitch, at the moment. But I have been looking at the values being generated by the wave converter and they are becoming unstable."

"Meaning?"

"Meaning that there is every chance that the field he has created could become larger; it could spread beyond the room."

"You mean the loop he has set up could take in the area immediately outside of the containment area, the one he originally programed?"

"Yes; and beyond."

"How far beyond?"

"Well... infinitely beyond."

Both studied the man on the screen. He was going through the same nervous ritual of hitting keys and checking the time. The knocking came again, but softer.

"That didn't sound as loud, did it?"

"No. I think that is because it is coming from further away; outside of the room."

"Outside of the..."

The screen flickered momentarily; then disappeared.

The being drifted into the chamber.

"I understand you have a problem..."

Sounds Abound

Sounds abound, and can be found,
With no option, or by choice.
From a piercing scream in a playground,
To the sadness in a voice.

A bird chirping in the dark.
The swishing of a broom.
The musical hum of a piano
Being moved from room to room.

The crackling of a burning log.
The ticking of a clock.
A cat scratching at a door.
Water trickling from a rock.

A twig breaking under foot.
A nail that's hammered in.
An egg frying in a pan.
The rolling of a bin.

The whimpering of a newborn pup.
Cans falling from a stack.
A slow fan moving heat around.
A train rattling down a track.

The roll of distant thunder.
A mower cutting grass.
The creaking of an ageing chair.
A tinkle of broken glass.

A fire truck's incessant wail.
The crack of a splitting branch.
Water hissing through a pipe.
A rumbling avalanche

The call of an oven's buzzer.
An ocean's steady lap.
A gunshot coming from a wood.
The splash of a dripping tap.

The whipping of a turbulent wind.
The hissing of a snake.
A boom box pounding in the street;
Soft rippling on a lake.

Branches quietly scraping together.
A motorcycle's roar.
The swelling sounds of a fledgling choir.
A cat scratching at the door.

The ringing of a garden chime.
The croak of a frog's deep call.
The strains of a distant song.
Echoes bouncing off a wall.

A radio in a passing car.
An aircraft's drone above.
Laughter sounding through a fence.
The cooing of a dove.

A church bell sending out a chime.
A flap of passing wings.
The roaring of a distant storm.
A bow's stroke tuning strings.

A motor car's blaring horn.
A quietly beating heart.
A wise old owl's haunting hoot.
An axle squeaking on a cart.

A lonely dog's plaintive howl.
The whisper of a breeze.
A distance runner's panting breath.
Raindrops bouncing in the trees.

The beating of a military drum.
A muffled baby's cry.
The strains of a Gregorian chant.
A lover's quiet sigh.

The flapping of a fluttering flag.
The scuff of dragging feet.
A special poem being read.
The chat when people meet.

Sounds abound, and can be found,
With no option or by choice.
Sounds abound, and can be found,
Giving life a voice.

In Pursuance of a God

Earthlings' never-ending quest;
The pursuance of a God.
Some with woven kneeling mats
Or a cross upon a rod.

There are so many ways to frame the quest,
With Christianity, Islam and Baha'i,
Jainism, Sikhism, Judaism and Shinto,
With countless others, by and by.

Through seeking light where there is darkness,
Finding a being that is everything.
Everything and always there.
One who sends emissaries into this shattered world,
To bring hope and make repair.

For some it's stained-glass windows
With candles, hymnals and pews;
With mumbled hymns and silent prayers
And holy dialogue, with cues.

As the earth spins through day and night,
The search for some great design
Moves ever on, seeking answers,
With which reason can align.

With religions misinterpreted;
With holy books misread;
With so many different houses of worship,
Who can see the way ahead?

Who or what is it that comes with such silent grace,
That builds stars and creates rivers that flow,
That reveals to followers the beauty of life,
When they seem to have nowhere to go?

Who or what commands such power,
Although it be ever so?
I for one are quite lost in its vastness;
And blessed are those who know.